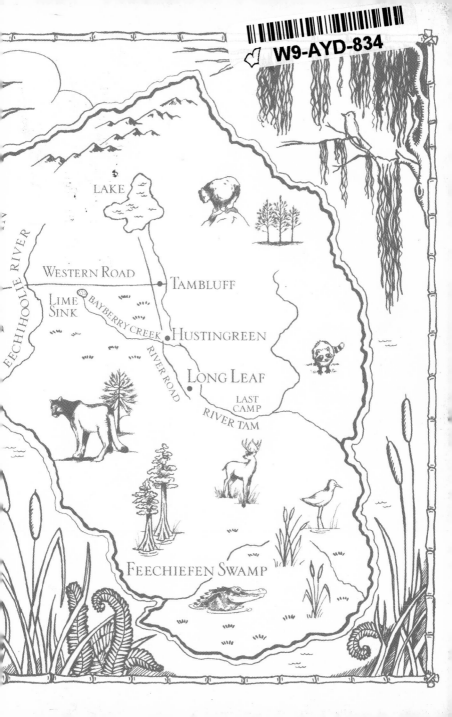

THE WILDERKING TRILOGY

The Bark of the Bog Owl

CORENWALD

JONATHAN ROGERS

BROADMAN
& HOLMAN
PUBLISHERS

NASHVILLE, TENNESSEE

0-8054-3131-4

Published by Broadman & Holman Publishers,
Nashville, Tennessee

Dewey Decimal Classification: F
Subject Headings: ADVENTURE FICTION
                    ADOLESCENCE—FICTION

Interior illustrations by Abe Goolsby
Map by Kristi Smith

1 2 3 4 5 6 7 8 9 10 08 07 06 05 04

For Lawrence and Gail Alligood,
patrons of the arts.

And for Lou Alice, of course.

Chapter One

The Bark
of the Bog Owl

His Majesty, King Darrow of Corenwald,
  Protector of the People,
  Defender of the Faith,
  Keeper of the Island
Tambluff Castle
West Bank of the River Tam
Tambluff, Corenwald

My Dearest King—

*You will be glad to learn that I am still available
for any quest, adventure, or dangerous mission
for which you might need a champion or knight-
errant. I specialize in dragon-slaying, but would
be happy to fight pirates or invading barbarians
if circumstances require. I would even be willing
to rescue a fair maiden imprisoned by evil
relatives. That would not be my first choice,
since I am not of marrying age. Still, in peaceful
and prosperous times like these, an adventurer
takes whatever work he can find.*

*As always, I am at your service and eagerly
await your reply.*

*Yours very sincerely,
Aidan Errolson of Longleaf Manor*

*P.S. I have not yet received an answer to my last
letter—or to my fourteen letters before that.
Mail service being what it is on the frontier, I
assume your replies were lost. I hope you don't
mind that I have taken the liberty of writing
again.*

Holding the stiff palmetto paper between ink-stained fingers, Aidan admired his letter one more time before rolling it and putting it back in his side pouch. The mail wagon wouldn't be by for another couple of days, and he thought it best to keep the letter on hand, in case another postscript came to him.

Besides being an avid letter-writer, Aidan Errolson was a warrior and an adventurer. He lived to ride with King Darrow's armies. He thrilled to hear the clank of plate armor, the bright ring of a sword unsheathed. He would rather sleep on a bedroll in a battle camp than in the finest bed in the finest castle in all of Corenwald.

At least, that's who he was on the inside. On the outside, Aidan was a shaggy-headed shepherd boy—a twelve-year-old bundle of knees and elbows in a homespun tunic and leather sandals. He had never had any real adventures. Being the son of one of Corenwald's great landholders, Aidan lived a comfortable and settled life.

And that, he believed, was the one great injustice of his otherwise happy existence.

Aidan came from a family of adventurers. His grandparents had been pioneers, among the earliest settlers of Corenwald's eastern frontier. When he was a younger man, Aidan's father Errol had been one of Corenwald's greatest warriors. He was still a teenager when he first marched out to battle to defend the kingdom that his forefathers had carved from the tanglewood.

By comparison, Aidan's peaceful, prosperous, civilized life seemed rather dull. True, this was what his grandparents had toiled for, what his parents had fought for. But Aidan wasn't sure the life of a shepherd suited him. Longleaf Manor, his father's vast estate, presented precious little opportunity for the sort of adventures that take place in real life, and not only in a boy's imagination.

That changed forever on the day Aidan first heard the bark of the bog owl.

‡ ‡ ‡

The first time Aidan heard the bark of the bog owl, he was tending sheep in the bottom pasture—or, rather, he was supposed to be tending sheep. In fact, he was dreaming the day away with little regard for his shepherdly duties. It was high spring, the sort of day that inspires a certain dreaminess in even the most earthbound and unimaginative of shepherd boys. Earlier in the day, a looming thunderhead had threatened to soak the bottom pasture. But it changed its mind and slid off to the south before dropping so much as a sprinkle on Aidan or his sheep. Now the clouds scudded across the blue like great bales of cotton under sail.

In the bottomlands that bordered the pasture, the forest birds were calling each to each. And even from where Aidan was, he could hear the zoom of a thousand bee wings darting and hovering above the little swamp lilies that carpeted the forest floor.

Of all the pastures on Longleaf Manor, the bottom pasture was Aidan's favorite. Situated at the farthest edge of the estate, it was a floodplain meadow of the River Tam, which formed the eastern boundary of Errol's lands. Here carefully tended fields and pastures, indeed all the gentle arts of cultivation, gave way again to wildness. Before him stretched a scene of pastoral tranquility: soft, fat sheep nibbled sweet spring grass, secure in their shepherd's care and undisturbed by any fear of danger. But behind him began a wilderness not very different from the one his forebears found when they first came to this country. There the red wolves still lurked beneath the moss-hung cypress and water oaks. Wildcats still prowled from limb to limb. And spring nights still resounded with the bellowing of great bull alligators summoning one another to battle.

Perched in the drooping elbow of a massive live oak, Aidan was composing a lullaby for his lambs:

The gator glides along the Tam
Just thirty strides away.
But fear thee not, my little lamb,
Your shepherd's here by night and day . . .

He was trying to work out a suitable refrain when he

was startled back to reality. From the treetops only a few feet behind him, the piercing call of a wild animal rose above the forest buzz and echoed across the meadow.

Ha-ha-ha-hrawffff-wooooooooo . . . Ha-ha-ha-hrawffff-wooooooooo.

It began as the sharp, short laugh of a monkey or hyena, then became a growling bark—almost as deep as a hound's bay—and finally a wolfish howl. If the wilderness could speak with a single voice, it would sound like this.

Ha-ha-ha-hrawffff-wooooooooo . . . Ha-ha-ha-hrawffff-wooooooooo.

It was the bark of the bog owl, and even though Aidan had never heard such a thing before, he couldn't mistake it for anything else. It spoke of wild places still untamed, of quests not yet pursued, of great deeds not yet done. Aidan's grandfather had spoken of it. He had heard the bark of the bog owl when he first came to Corenwald from the old country. But as families like Aidan's settled and civilized this wild island, the bog owls pushed deeper into the swamps and marshes to the south and east.

Ha-ha-ha-hrawffff-wooooooooo . . . Ha-ha-ha-hrawffff-wooooooooo.

Aidan was more than startled; he was thrilled straight through. An adventurer's heart beat wildly against his ribs. He felt himself to be the person he had always hoped he was: not a shepherd boy who wished he were a soldier, but a soldier who happened to be playing the part of a shepherd boy.

Aidan couldn't sit still. He had to do something—something adventurous. Seeing movement on the far edge of the meadow, he leaped from the tree limb, crouching as he pulled sling and stone from his side pouch. A bear skulking near his sheep! Actually, it was a clump of blackberry briars about the size of a bear; but it served Aidan's purpose well enough. He whirled the stone about his head and let fly, scoring a hit on the imaginary predator's head. Wheeling to his right, he slew two suspiciously wolfish-looking tree stumps before they could flee his lethal stones. He then took up his shepherd's staff with both hands like a broadsword. He hacked and jabbed at trees and bushes, thrusting, parrying, and lunging, battling through imaginary foes. Triumphantly, he mounted a high stump in a single leap.

Feeling full of himself, Aidan composed another song on the spot—not a lullaby this time but a soldier's march. He turned toward the tangled forest—toward the bog owl's hidden perch—and sang this song of himself:

Aidan of the Tam I am,
The youngest son of Errol.
With sling and stone and staff alone
I guard my flocks from peril.

Aidan of the Tam I am,
I know no fear of danger.
Though I am young, my arm is strong.
I dread not beast or stranger.

Aidan of the Tam I am,
A liegeman true of Darrow.
The kingdom's foes I will oppose
With sword and spear and arrow.

He leaped from the stump, raised his staff over his head like a battle flag, and, whooping the Corenwald war cry, made a charge through the middle of the flock. The sheep scattered madly before him, bleating and bumping. Their eyes were white-rimmed with fright.

He circled back at a dead run and galloped along the forest's edge toward a little creek that hurried across the meadow on its way to the Tam. He planted the end of his staff on the creek bank and, intending to vault to the other side, flung his feet skyward and pushed off from the staff's handle with all his strength.

Aidan had never actually pole-vaulted before. And, as is often the case with first attempts, this one ended in disaster. Instead of making a smooth arc over the creek as he had envisioned, he went into a careening somersault and crashed into the mud on the far side of the creek.

His adventurous spirit was extinguished as suddenly as it had been awakened. Mumbling, he plucked himself out of the mud and was poking around for broken bones when he thought he heard a giggle. He looked back at the sheep. Most of them were looking at him curiously, convinced that he had gone quite mad. But sheep don't giggle. Aidan had spent many hours with these very sheep, and he was sure there was not a giggler among them. Besides, now that he thought about it, the giggling had come from above, perhaps from the beech tree that overhung the creek.

As Aidan peered quizzically into the treetop, the air was split by another wild cry: *Ha-ha-ha-hrawffff-wooooooooo . . . Ha-ha-ha-hrawffff-wooooooooo.* The bog owl! Somewhere in the beech tree sat the most mysterious and elusive of the creatures that teemed in Corenwald's vast forests. Nobody Aidan knew—not even his grandfather—had ever so much as seen a bog owl, though everybody claimed to know somebody who knew somebody who had. Yet here he was, in broad daylight, only a few feet away from one. He was determined to get a good look at it.

The tree had its full growth of spring leaves. Aidan had no chance of seeing the owl as long as it stayed in the treetop; he knew he had to make it fly. He picked up a small white pebble and threw it up into the crown of the tree where he thought the owl was hiding. There was no movement—not so much as the slight rustle of the pebble falling back through the leaves. The pebble seemed to have gotten stuck in the treetop.

When Aidan bent down to find a second rock for another try, something bounded off the back of his head and into the grass beside him. It was the white pebble, apparently dislodged by a breeze in the treetop. Thinking little of it, Aidan continued his search.

He picked up a slightly bigger rock, a red piece of gravel a little larger than a robin's egg, and threw it toward the bog owl's perch. To Aidan's surprise, this rock lodged in the treetop too.

Aidan realized it would take a larger rock to flush the bog owl—one too heavy to get stuck among the leaves of a beech tree. When he bent down to find one, again he felt something hard bounce off the back of his head. It was a little red piece of gravel—the same one he had thrown into the tree. "That's strange," muttered Aidan. "What are the chances?" He soon found just the rock he needed: a brown, flat creek stone about the size of his palm. He cast it up among the leaves and stepped back a few paces, having no desire to get hit on the head again. No owl emerged, but Aidan was relieved to see the rock drop back to earth, according to the generally accepted laws of gravity.

Only it wasn't the same rock. Leaning over to pick it up where it lay, Aidan saw that the rock that had dropped from the tree was gray and squarish, not brown and flat. As he stood marveling at this turn of events, he found the flat rock—or rather, it found him. Whistling down from the treetop, it cracked him squarely on the head.

Aidan's anger rose along with the knot on his head. Then the tree began to shake, and a high, whinnying laugh rose from its branches. Aidan's mouth dropped open. His eyes bulged. He took a few steps backward, but as he turned to run from the enchanted tree, his feet got tangled and he fell flat.

Aidan managed to raise himself to a sitting position, but before he could get to his feet, the lower branches of the tree rustled again, and a strange creature dropped to the ground only a few strides away. Crouched on all fours, it appeared to be as big as Aidan himself. The creature was covered with large, reptilian scales like an alligator's. A long, thick, ridged tail trailed behind; its hard, bony skull was covered with a dozen or more pyramid-shaped lumps. It fixed a menacing glare on Aidan as it crept slowly toward him. Fear paralyzed him. This was more wildness than he had bargained for.

Chapter Two

The Wilderking Chant

Jasper and Percy, the Errolson twins, were supposed to be repairing the grape arbor near the manor house. But the rhythmic clanging that sounded from underneath the draping scuppernong vines was the ring of broadsword on broadsword, not the ring of hammer on spike.

The twins had just turned fifteen and were now eligible for service in the Corenwalder army. So all of their spare time—and much of their work time, too, as it turned out—they spent drilling and practicing, sharpening the skills of swordsmanship and cavalry. In this particular duel, it was Percy's turn to play the foreign invader, a black-armored, black-hearted knight of the hated Pyrthen Empire. Jasper, fighting for Corenwald and King Darrow, was getting the better of him. Percy broke and ran (the Pyrthen always broke and ran in the Errolsons' military exercises), and Jasper ran after him with raised sword.

"Fly, Pyrthen swine!" called Jasper, "and never set foot on this island again. This is Corenwald, free and true!" He picked up a rock and threw it in his brother's direction. "Go tell that to Emperor Mareddud!"

Laughing and running down the cart path, Percy suddenly stopped. Jasper looked to see what had so arrested his brother's attention. A tall, barrel-chested old man was approaching up the cart path with long, rapid strides. Bright white hair erupted from his head in all directions. His long white beard was equally rambunctious. Two goats, a billy and a nanny, trotted behind him. The Errolsons leaned on their swords and watched the visitor as he approached.

The old man carried no walking stick. He was dressed in a dusty tan robe, and, though it was only May, the hot Corenwald sun had already browned his skin to a deep cinnamon. But the most remarkable thing about the man's appearance was his pale green eyes. Even from twenty strides away, the Errolsons could see that these were not the eyes of a normal man. When the old man fixed his gaze on Jasper and Percy, they weren't quite sure if he saw them or not; he seemed to be looking through them.

When he was five strides from the Errolson twins, the man stopped so abruptly that the goats ran into the back of his legs. Gazing into—or through—the Errolsons' eyes, the old man spoke: "I am here to find the king."

The twins exchanged a look. Was the old bird off his perch? Percy spoke first. "I'm afraid you've overshot it, Grandfather. King Darrow's palace is a half-day's march up the River Road, the way you came."

"I am here to find the king," the old man repeated. "He dwells in the House of Errol."

"You've come to the House of Errol," said Jasper. "We are Errol's sons. But no king is here."

Percy could never resist a joke. "Perhaps you're look-ing for the House of Merrill," he teased. "His place is just west of here. But he's only a chicken farmer, so I don't see why the king would be there."

The brothers laughed at Percy's joke, but if the old man heard it, he gave no indication. The boys' laughter was cut short when the front door swung open and their father Errol clattered down the steps. They stared in amazement as their father dropped to his knees and kissed the callused hand of the unknown wayfarer. They could make no sense of it. Their father was one of the Four and Twenty Noblemen of Corenwald, one of King Darrow's closest advisers, yet he was paying homage to this dusty stranger who, from the looks of things, didn't have the sense God gave a snapping turtle. Errol's eyes were wet with tears as he spoke. "Reverend friend and teacher, you are most welcome to my house."

The old man patted Errol's head, but he didn't speak or otherwise move. The nanny goat snuffled at Errol's hair, trying to decide whether to eat it.

"Father!" Jasper marveled. "Do you know this madman?"

Percy broke in. "He thinks we've got King Darrow hidden somewhere."

Errol rose to his feet and glared at his sons. "You will speak respectfully of this man! He is worthy of your honor. He is Bayard the Truthspeaker, Corenwald's greatest prophet!"

If the twins were amazed before, there were no words for their astonishment now. This man was Bayard the Truthspeaker? The great prophet and counselor their father and grandfather had spoken of so often? Had he come to this, tramping around the countryside in the company of goats, babbling nonsense?

Errol turned back to Bayard. "It has been twenty years since you last visited this house. To what do we owe this happy honor?"

Bayard pierced Errol with those green eyes and said in a low tone, "I am here to find the king who dwells in the House of Errol."

Errol blushed slightly and cleared his throat. He glanced at his sons, then looked down at his hands for a few awkward seconds. "What am I thinking?" he suddenly said, with a forced smile. "The sun is blistering. Please, Bayard, come inside and take some refreshment."

Leaving everyone behind, the old man headed up the stairs leading to the entry hall, taking the steps two at a time. The goats had already mounted the first step when Percy caught them by the horns, one with each hand. "Hold on there, Billy. Hold on, Nan! Where do you think you're going?"

Bayard stopped on the sixth step but did not turn around: "They go where I go."

Percy looked to his father. "In that case," said Errol with a broadening smile, "they are heartily welcome in my house." Shaking his head in wonderment, Percy let go of the goats' horns, and they scrambled up the steps to catch up with their master.

Errol spoke to the three baffled servants who had watched the scene through the entry-hall window. One scurried to the kitchen, and the other two ran out the front door. "Let's retire to the great room," directed Errol. "What other room is suitable for so great a guest?

Jasper, Percy, you will join us; I have sent servants to fetch your brothers."

In the great room, Errol placed Bayard in the seat of honor near the huge stone fireplace. The goats sat on the floor, on either side of his chair. Errol and his two sons sat in chairs across from Bayard. The efficient servant arrived immediately with a tray of refreshments and placed it on the hearth beside the old prophet. On the tray were a pitcher of ale for Bayard, a pitcher of water for the goats, three drinking bowls, and a plate of cheese.

"Goat cheese," offered Errol, suddenly embarrassed. Bayard gave no indication that he had heard him. He poured a bowl of ale and sniffed it. Closing his eyes, he took a sip and nodded approvingly. Then, to the amazement of everyone in the room, he set the ale on the floor in front of the billy goat, who began lapping it eagerly. He poured a second bowl of ale for the nanny. For himself, he poured a bowl of water. He left the cheese untouched.

After a painful silence, Errol addressed his sons. "Bayard here was a friend of your grandfather's. When they first came to this part of the country, it was nothing but swamp and tanglewood, ruled by panthers, bears, and wolves." Bayard said nothing; he appeared not to be listening. The billy goat lapped up the last of his ale and burped loud and long.

Errol soldiered on. "Boys, that was a generation of great pioneers. They carved a civilization out of pure wilderness—a place where they wouldn't answer to any tyrant, only to their consciences and to the God who made them free men."

The old wayfarer seemed perfectly unaware of anyone

else in the room. Jasper and Percy were embarrassed for their father. They had never seen him so thunderstruck, not even in the presence of King Darrow himself.

After another awkward pause, Errol continued. "I've known Bayard all my life. When I first marched out to battle against the Pyrthens—I was about your age—it was Bayard here who pronounced the benediction on the troops."

Not so much as a flicker of recognition passed across the old man's face. The nanny goat was chewing thoughtfully on a hanging tapestry that had been in Errol's family for generations. But at least she seemed to be listening. Percy cast a sidelong glance out the window, hoping that his brothers would soon arrive from the fields. Brennus, the eldest brother, always seemed to know what to say and do. But then again, so did Father, yet Bayard the Truthspeaker was proving to be more than he could handle.

Errol was still droning on, "And when the people of Corenwald decided they wanted a king, who do you think placed the crown on Darrow's head?" There was a brief silence, and Percy realized his father was looking directly at him, expecting an answer.

"Bayard?" Percy's answer sounded unsure, like a question, even though his father had told him this story a hundred times.

"The very same! And he remained Darrow's chief adviser until—" here Errol stopped short. "Well . . . ahem . . . in any case, the point is, you, my sons, are in the presence of Corenwald's greatest man—King Darrow excepted, of course."

Jasper and Percy looked closely at the old visitor. One of his goats was tugging at the sleeve of his robe. The other was chewing on his sandal. He certainly didn't look like Corenwald's greatest man, with his white hair and beard shooting off in all directions, and those green eyes staring off into the distance.

Their thoughts were interrupted when two more young men entered the room. They were Brennus and Maynard, the eldest two of the Errolson boys, just in from the hayfield. They had been scything the season's first hay crop, side by side with the hired hands. Still covered with dust and sweat, Brennus and Maynard stood blinking in the dim light of the great room.

Errol was about to introduce the new arrivals when Bayard rose to his feet. Still gazing well past his audience, he began to chant a verse that all Corenwalders knew. It was the Wilderking Chant—an ancient prophecy, as old as Corenwald itself:

When fear of God has left the land,
To be replaced by fear of man;
When Corenwalders free and true
Enslave themselves and others too,
When mercy and justice disappear,
When life is cheap and gold is dear,
When freedom's flame has burned to ember
And Corenwalders can't remember
What are truths and what are lies,
Then will the Wilderking arise.

To the palace he comes from forests and swamps.
Watch for the Wilderking!
Leading his troops of wild men and brutes.

16

Watch for the Wilderking!
He will silence the braggart,
  ennoble the coward.
Watch for the Wilderking!
Justice will roll, and mercy will toll.
Watch for the Wilderking!
He will guard his dear lambs with the
  staff of his hand.
Watch for the Wilderking!
With a stone he shall quell the panther fell.
Watch for the Wilderking!
Watch for the Wilderking, widows and orphans.
Look to the swamplands, ye misfit, ye outcast.
From the land's wildest places a wild man will come
To give the land back to her people.

Bayard looked into Errol's eyes. "I am here to see the Wilderking of Corenwald. He dwells in the House of Errol."

For the first time, Errol felt himself losing patience with the old man. Errol was a great patriot, and his loyalty to the king was unshakable. "Speak no more of any king but Darrow. Darrow is king of Corenwald, and he dwells not here. I have pledged my allegiance to Darrow; I have risked my life for Darrow; it is by Darrow's pleasure that I hold these lands. And any man who raises himself up against King Darrow will learn what my sword is made of."

Bayard seemed entirely indifferent to Errol's outburst. He paced across the room and stood before Brennus. He studied the eldest Errolson from his head down to his boots and back up again. At twenty years old, Brennus certainly cut the most kingly figure of all the brothers. He was tall and handsome. He carried himself with an air of command. He was accustomed to getting his way.

Bayard nodded his head. "Your name is Brennus, the eldest son of Errol, by rights the heir to Longleaf. But in your bones you feel that you were born for greater things." Brennus shifted nervously, uncomfortable at having his secret ambitions spoken in front of his family.

Bayard continued, "Indeed, I see a regal bearing in your face. You are strong of limb, adroit with sword and shield. Men would rejoice to follow such a leader."

The old prophet gave Brennus one more look, as if arriving at his final assessment: "But you, Brennus, are not the Wilderking."

Bayard turned next to Maynard, the second brother. In all things, Maynard was second to Brennus: second in age (he was eighteen), second in stature, second in talents. Convinced that he would never quite measure up to his elder brother, Maynard had sharpened the skills of cunning. His eyes were permanently narrow from a lifetime of scheming.

Bayard began, "You are Maynard, Errol's second son. You know the prize does not always go to the one who is first by birth or first in ability, first in strength, or first in the field. Sometimes the prize—even the prize of a throne—goes to the one who has learned to put himself first, even if birth and talents have not. This you have learned to do, Maynard." Maynard averted his gaze, angry at having been so revealed, but even still, a greedy glint was visible in his eyes. Bayard continued, "But you are not the Wilderking."

Bayard faced the twins. "The twins I have met already: Jasper and Percy. Jasper, you are the scholar of the family. Only fifteen years old, yet you surpass even your father in the lore and history of Corenwald. Every prophecy you have learned by heart, and every date, every battle, every family of note in the kingdom. This is the knowledge that serves a ruler well. A king must know his kingdom." Jasper stood a little taller; a smile of pride played about the corners of his mouth. "And yet, you are not the Wilderking."

Bayard turned to Jasper's twin brother. "That leaves only Percy, does it not?" Percy could not believe what he was hearing. He had always been viewed as the family's underachiever. His only real accomplishment had been to maintain a wry grin, almost without interruption, for all of his fifteen years. Could he possibly be the Wilderking?

"You, Percy, may not have much up here," Bayard tapped Percy's forehead with a gnarled forefinger, "but here," he pointed at Percy's heart, "here, Percy, you will surpass your brothers." The old prophet's face softened into a smile. "But you must learn not to mock and tease the aged wayfarer who comes to your door."

Bayard turned to Errol. A perplexed expression clouded the old man's face. "Errol, I do not see the Wilderking among your sons."

Errol's relief was obvious. His old friend seemed to be returning to his senses. "Well, Bayard, now that we've settled that, let's sit down to a proper meal together, shall we?" He nudged a goat aside and put his arm around Bayard.

Bayard didn't seem quite satisfied. "But, Errol, do you have another son?"

Errol stopped and counted his sons, his lips moving slightly. "But of course I have another son! How could I have forgotten? Aidan, my youngest, is tending sheep in the bottom pasture."

"I wish to see him."

"Certainly, of course! He would be heartbroken if he missed Bayard the Truthspeaker. I shall send for him at once."

The faraway look returned to Bayard's eyes, much to Errol's alarm. "No, Bayard," he began, "hold on a minute. You've got the wrong idea." One of the brothers snickered. All four were trying not to laugh.

Chapter Three
Dobro Turtlebane

Set upon by a terrible tree monster, Aidan's courage failed him completely. He went cross-eyed with panic as the crouching beast got closer. When it was only one stride away, it raised up on its hind legs and stood upright over him. Just when Aidan was sure he would faint from sheer terror, the wind shifted and the creature's astonishing smell hit him like a wave. It was a fishy, slippery smell, sharpened by the pungent odor of wild onions and rancid berries. It was a horrible, eye-watering smell, and it revived Aidan from his swoon like a whiff of smelling salts.

Aidan's vision began to clear, and he could see that despite the scaly skin and long tail, the monster's form and movements were almost human. Beneath that terrifying bony crown, the creature's face, for all its wild ferocity, was almost boylike. Aidan shook the last of the cobwebs from his head.

The monster *was* a boy! He was unlike any boy Aidan had ever seen, but he was a boy nevertheless. He didn't have a many-pointed skull; that was a helmet made from the shell of a snapping turtle. He wore a tunic made from a whole alligator hide; that explained the scales and the tail. The tunic was cinched at the waist with a cottonmouth snake, held fast with its own fangs rather than a belt buckle. From his waist dangled a side pouch fashioned from the wedge-shaped head of an alligator garfish.

Aidan rose to his feet. The wild boy was a head shorter than Aidan and skinnier too—not puny but a wiry, tough sort of skinny. His skin was a grayish-brown, though Aidan couldn't tell if his skin was actually that color or only coated with river mud. The boy's face was pinched and fierce, and his eyes stared wild and unblinking beneath a single long eyebrow.

Aidan had never seen such a person, but he thought he knew what he was. He was one of the feechiefolk. Aidan's grandfather had told him many tales of this wild, nomadic tribe that traveled up and down Corenwald's many rivers and swamps. These creatures were equally comfortable in the water or in treetops and were rarely seen by "civilizers," as they called the Corenwalders. According to Aidan's grandfather, feechies had an uncanny, almost magical ability to disappear into the forest or under the water anytime settlers were nearby. He had described their fierce, warlike spirit but also their unquenchable jollity. But then again, Grandfather had often invented wild tales to entertain his grandchildren.

The house servants often threatened to throw him to the feechiefolk when he misbehaved, but Aidan had always assumed the feechiefolk were imaginary creatures, like leprechauns or boogiemen. Yet here before him stood what appeared to be an actual feechie boy. Aidan had no idea what this wild boy might do next. He was fierce—no question about it—but not exactly threatening. On the other hand, he didn't appear to be friendly either. He was just wild; there was no other way to describe him.

The two boys regarded one another. At last the wild boy's nasally voice broke the silence. "Are we going to tangle or not?"

Aidan stood flabbergasted. It had never occurred to him that this wild child of the river bottoms might speak a recognizable language. The feechie boy placed his hands on his hips and leaned in closer. "You heard me, young civilizer. Let's tangle."

Aidan blinked twice, not quite sure he understood. "T-tangle? Do you mean fight? You want to fight?"

"Sure, I reckon!" answered the river boy, bending into a slight crouch and raising his fists in front of him. For the first time a little smile flickered on his muddy face.

Aidan swallowed hard. He wasn't feeling quite as wild and adventurous as he had a little while earlier. "Wh-why would we want to fight?"

The river boy straightened up and cocked his head. He seemed genuinely perplexed. "You want a reason? For fighting? Hmmm . . . I reckon I could think of something."

He scratched his head with one hand, counted on his fingers with the other, and after a short pause looked up again. "All right. Here goes. But I ain't had a chance to polish it up yet, so don't laugh." He hummed a little to get his pitch, then sang to the same march tune Aidan had sung a few minutes earlier:

Dobro of the Tam I am
And I could whip you easy.
I'll make you weep cause you smell like sheep,
And your looks are kind of greasy.

The verse was not up to Aidan's standards, of course, but Dobro of the Tam seemed proud of it. "See," he said, "you not the only rhyme-maker on this river." A self-satisfied smile showed several greenish teeth, as well as three gaps where greenish teeth should have been.

Aidan thought he caught a glimpse of the feechie good humor his grandfather had told him about. The river boy was smiling. That was a good sign, wasn't it? Perhaps he could escape without getting torn limb from limb. On the surface, Dobro's song was a challenge and an insult, but for some reason it had put Aidan at ease. It was a funny song, made funnier by Dobro's ridiculous gap-toothed grin. Being a poet himself, Aidan appreciated the wild boy's effort. And considering it was spur-of-the-moment, it wasn't all that bad.

"Good work," Aidan laughed. He was starting to like this fellow, in spite of his boorish behavior. "But I'm surprised you'd make fun of *my* looks. You look like you were fished up from the river mud. And I may smell like sheep, but you smell like a . . . like a . . . well, you smell like you brush your teeth with mashed garlic. You smell like you use a rotten catfish for a pillow." Aidan was only warming up. "You smell like you slick your hair with eel slime."

Aidan had meant for his remarks to be friendly ribbing, the way a boy might make fun of a friend's new haircut or his too-clean tunic. He had no way of knowing he had just completed the ceremonial *rudeswap* that usually precedes a feechie fight. If there had been a slim hope of Dobro leaving without a fight, that hope just got slimmer.

The wild boy creased his brow into the fiercest scowl he could manage and pulled down the corners of his mouth until his bottom lip poked out farther than his nose. His pointed ears showed red, even through the mud, and he began to hop circles around Aidan, his knuckled fists flying in wild gyrations around his head.

"You done it now. Dobro Turtlebane's going to bust your flapper. Raise them turkey wings to a defensive posture. I won't strike a man who ain't defending hisself. So come on. Put 'em up."

Despite his slight build, Dobro Turtlebane did cut a fearsome figure. What he lacked in size, he more than made up for in enthusiasm. He seemed fully capable of whipping a man twice his size. And yet, in spite of the looming danger, Aidan was still more amused than frightened. He chuckled at this river wasp, who continued to buzz around him, bobbing and darting and dodging, impatient for Aidan to assume a fighting stance.

"Now come on," barked Dobro. "Let's get this here tussle started."

Aidan stood his ground but didn't raise his fists. "There's not going to be any tussle. If you're mad at me for throwing rocks at you, I'm sorry. I thought you were somebody else. And besides," he added, rubbing the knot on his head, "you got the better of that deal already. You seem decent enough. I'd rather make friends than fight."

"You're kind to say so," answered Dobro, who continued to weave and dance. "I like you too. But that's got nothing to do with it. Stop changing the subject, and let's proceed to the fisticuffs."

Aidan was not at all sure how he was going to get out of this mess. The feechie boy seemed determined to fight him, with or without a good reason. "I've got no cause. And besides," he added in a quieter tone, for now he got closer to the heart of the matter, "I'm not much of a fighter."

At this, Dobro stood still. He stared in disbelief, his shoulders slightly slumped, "Hold on, hold on, hold on," he began. "I know you a tough one. You said so yourself."

"No, I didn't!" said Aidan indignantly. He was convinced that the river boy was picking a fight on false premises.

"Sure you did," the wild boy answered. "You said you are not afraid of beasts or strangers and you fight for the kingdom with a bow and arrow."

Aidan looked perplexedly at Dobro.

"Now don't go denying it," said the river boy impatiently. "You stood right there on that stump for me and all creation to see, and you said you was young and your arm was strong, and you liked to fight."

It dawned on Aidan that Dobro was talking about the song he had sung while still under the emboldening influence of the bark of the bog owl.

"But that was just a song. It was make-believe. I've never even been in a real fight."

Dobro whistled. His fierceness was mostly gone now, and there was a touch of pity in his voice. "Well, maybe we could have just a short little fight? I won't disfigure you very much."

"No. I don't want to fight." Aidan's adventurous

spirit had ebbed away, and he felt the burn of embarrassment on his cheeks.

"Well, if you've never tried it," answered Dobro, trying to sound like he was the sensible one, "how can you say you don't want to?"

Aidan turned and walked toward the middle of the pasture. "I need to tend to my sheep."

Dobro hopped to catch up with him. "Maybe we could just box."

"No."

"Want to rassle?"

"You got the wrong person. I'm just a shepherd boy. Climb your tree and leave me alone."

Aidan continued stalking off toward his sheep. But he was stopped by a wailing cry behind him. "*Aaaaaawwww haaawwww haaawwww haaawwww! Aaaaaawwww haaawwww haaawwww haaawwww!*" He turned around and saw Dobro dropped to his knees, his face contorted into a sobbing grimace.

He rushed to the wild boy's side. "What happened? Are you snakebit? Did you twist your ankle?"

"*Aaaaaawwww haaawwww haaawwww haaawwww!*"

"Are you hurt? What's the matter?"

Dobro continued to howl. His attempts to answer were choked out by loud sobs. Finally he spoke: "Ev-ev-ever since my brothers gone downriver, I got nobody to fight with." He broke off and sniffed loud and long. "It's just so lo-ho-ho-honesome. *Aaaaawwwww!*"

"You are trying to pick a fight because you are lonesome?"

Dobro nodded his head. "I just needed a friend. That's all."

"That's how you make friends?"

"You got any better ideas?"

"Well, I . . ."

"I see you chunking rocks with that slinger and cutting and jobbing that whacker stick. I hear you singing that song about fighting and carrying on, and I says to myself, 'Dobro, there's a civilizer with some spirit and gumption. We got all the same hobbies.' So I clumb down to introduce myself and make friends."

Dobro looked like he was about to start crying again, but he managed to go on. "And you go making me feel lower than a mud turtle. Mama's right about your kind of people."

"What's my kind of people?" asked Aidan.

"Civilizers. I'm not supposed to go near a civilizer. Mama says you folks'll civilize us all to sorrow and misery. If she finds out about this, I'm in the deep mud."

Dobro turned back toward the forest. "You probably right. It's time for me to go back up the tree."

Aidan felt rotten for having rejected Dobro's friendly gestures, even if they were the most unusual offer of friendship he had ever received. He didn't want to see the feechie boy go. As Dobro reached the beech tree, Aidan spoke up: "Before you leave, can I ask you one thing?"

"I reckon so."

"Do you want to wrestle?"

Chapter Four

A Wrestling Match

Dobro's muddy face brightened at Aidan's challenge. "Do I want to rassle?" he squealed. "Of course I do!"

Before Aidan knew what was happening, the feechie boy had dashed over, knocked him to the ground, and attached himself to Aidan's head with a wrenching head-lock.

"Wait, Dobro, wait," sputtered Aidan. "I wasn't ready yet. Let go a minute. We need to discuss the ground rules."

Dobro released him. "I already know the ground rules. We throw each other on the ground. Them's the rules."

"I mean we have to agree on what's allowed and what's not allowed—tackling, tripping, choke holds—things like that."

Dobro looked bewildered. Was the civilizer teasing him? He couldn't imagine any sort of wrestling that didn't involve tackling, tripping, and choke holds. As a matter of fact, most feechie dance steps involved at least one or two of those things.

"Next thing," said Dobro, "you'll say there's no bit-ing or head-butting or eye-poking. I thought we was having a rassling match not a sewing party." Actually, this was a bad example; biting and head-butting were quite common at feechie sewing parties.

After a long negotiation, Aidan and Dobro settled on a hybrid sort of wrestling—half-civilized, half-feechie—in which tripping, tackling, hair-pulling, and head-butting were legal, eye-poking was prohibited, and biting was allowed only as a last resort.

When the wrestling began, it was a frantic affair. The opponents rolled and tumbled and careened across the pasture like two wildcats, one cannoning through the air, then the other. Arms and legs flailed in every direction as the two boys struggled. Aidan was an experienced wrestler, but he had not seen anything like Dobro. The feechie boy was extremely strong for his size and impossibly quick. He twisted and spun like a tornado, yet never seemed to lose control of his limbs. He clearly knew what he was doing.

Nevertheless, Aidan held his own well enough. He had a significant advantage in both height and weight, and being the youngest of five brothers had taught him to be resourceful against superior opponents. Also, he was tougher than he looked. Still, Aidan suspected that the feechie boy could finish him off anytime he wanted. Dobro was toying with him a little. He didn't want to cut short such an excellent wrestling match; he was having too much fun. For that matter, so was Aidan.

Dobro had just thrown Aidan into the little creek and was grinding his face in the mud when they heard a stampede of hooves behind them, and the frantic bleats of the sheep: "Baaaaaaaaaah! Baaaaaaaaaah! *Baaaaaaaaaah!*"

Aidan and Dobro scanned the pasture to see what had troubled the sheep. At first, Aidan saw nothing, but Dobro elbowed him and pointed toward a brush pile at the forest's edge. There crouched a panther ready to spring—not an imaginary predator this time but a real panther, with tan fur and big, meaty paws, about six feet long with another three feet of tail. He had fierce golden eyes, black twitchy ears, sharp white teeth, and a long pink tongue, which at that moment was licking his chops. He seemed unable to decide which of the pretty lambs would be tastiest.

Aidan fumbled for his sling, hoping to get a stone off before the big cat pounced. But Dobro scrambled up the creek bank. "What fun!" he shouted. "I ain't never fought a panther before!" He snatched up Aidan's staff from under the beech tree and charged recklessly toward the panther.

From the corner of his golden eye, the cat saw Dobro coming and twisted around to face him. It bared its fangs and wailed a deep, rumbling moan that became a piercing scream. Still, the wild boy came on, answering the panther's cry with the exuberant, singsong battle yell of the feechiefolk: *"Haaaaaaa-wwwwwweeeeeeee!"*

The panther was back on its haunches, its ears flat against its head, when Dobro thwacked Aidan's staff sharply between its eyes. Aidan had never seen such fearlessness—or foolhardiness, as it turned out. A full-grown panther was not easily intimidated, even by a staff-wielding lizard boy. In fact, a blow from a shepherd's staff was just enough to make a panther good and angry. The cat reared up on its hind legs to make a lunge. Dobro gave it one more whack in the ribs, then dropped the staff and tore out across the pasture, back the way he came.

By this time, Aidan had his sling and stone at the ready. He raised the sling and whirled it around his head. Dobro's eyes were wild, but he wore a foolish grin. The panther was gaining on him.

The sling whistled around Aidan's head, but he didn't have a shot. Dobro was between Aidan and the panther, directly in the stone's path. The panther was closer still. Dobro still had that insane grin as he pumped his arms and legs as hard as he could.

Aidan summoned all his powers of concentration. He would get only one shot at the panther, one chance to rescue his new friend. Having reached its full speed, the cat was a tan blur; it would be on Dobro in a blink. At the tiniest opening, Aidan would have to release the stone.

Just when the panther got close enough to strike, Dobro threw himself to the ground in a flying somersault. The panther leaped to pounce on him. This was the opening Aidan was looking for. He let fly. The stone whistled through the air and cracked into the panther's skull just below the ear. The cat screamed a sharp shriek of pain, then thudded heavily on top of Dobro's crouching form. The panther was dead.

Aidan's legs felt like rubber as he staggered over to the motionless heap of panther and feechie boy. The cat moved, and Aidan instinctively reached for another stone. But he quickly realized that Dobro was trying to hoist the panther off his back. Aidan pulled the big cat off and helped Dobro to his feet. "Wooo!" said Dobro. "That rascal's heavy." He was still grinning that same grin.

"Y-y-you all right, Dobro?"

Dobro looked puzzled. "Course I'm all right. I ain't the one got hit with a rock." He was dusting off his gator-skin tunic. "Yes sir, Aidan of the Tam, I'd say we make a good panther-killing team. Dobro draws him out, Aidan knocks him down."

"You don't mean you were *trying* to make the panther chase you?"

"Sure I was. I seen you hit them stumps from a hundred yards away, but I figured if you was going to hit a moving target, we'd need to draw it a little closer."

"But what if I had missed?"

"You wasn't going to miss. You got what it takes, that's easy to see. Even if you *are* a civilizer."

A distant voice was calling from beyond the next pasture. "Aidan! Aidan!" One of the house servants was running toward them. "Aidan! Run home at once!"

"That's just Ebbe," said Aidan, turning toward Dobro. "You'll like him." But the feechie boy had disappeared. One civilizer at a time was more than enough for Dobro.

Aidan turned around, looking for Dobro in all directions. Not seeing him, he shrugged his shoulders and trotted toward the manor house.

When Aidan met Ebbe in the next pasture, the old servant gave him a perplexed stare. The tussle with Dobro had left Aidan a mess. His face was scratched and streaked with mud, his hair was in muddy disarray, and one eye was swollen. His wet tunic was ripped, and his knees and elbows were skinned. Ebbe looked him over from head to toe, then back up again. "Aidan," he said at last, "what happened to you?"

"Well, first there was a bog owl," Aidan began excitedly. "Then Dobro jumped out of the tree, and we had a wrestling match, but a panther came out of the woods and—"

"Ah, forget I asked," the grouchy old servant interrupted. "I don't have any idea what you're talking about. Your father is waiting for you at the big house. It sounded important, so you'd better run along, young flibbertigibbet. I'll look after the sheep."

Aidan ran along, stung by Ebbe's insult. "Flibbertigibbet!" he muttered to himself. "We'll see who's a flibbertigibbet when Ebbe sees the panther I killed in the bottom pasture!"

Chapter Five

Hail to the Wilderking

When Aidan entered the manor house, the door to the great hall was open, and he could hear his brothers speaking in low tones within. He stood outside the door to listen.

The first voice Aidan could make out was that of Brennus. "You're being ridiculous. None of us is the Wilderking."

"Yes, but what if one of us were . . ." It was Percy.

"He's going to come from the wild places," said Jasper. "From the swamps and the marshes and the forests. That's why he's called the Wilderking."

Maynard interrupted. "Look around, brother. You live on a great estate. You have a dozen house servants. You're no Wilderking."

"I didn't say *I* was the Wilderking, Maynard. I just said what if one of us was. Besides, doesn't the prophecy say the Wilderking guards his lambs with a staff? We've all done that."

"So has every ten-year-old in Corenwald," shot back Maynard. "The prophecy also says the Wilderking will slay a panther with a stone. When did any of us do that?" Out in the hallway, Aidan gasped.

Jasper, a great student of the Wilderking prophecy, spoke in the authoritative tone he reserved for his little lectures. "You're being too literal anyway, Percy. Most scholars say those lines are figurative." One of the brothers groaned. This was a common reaction when Jasper started talking. Jasper seemed not to notice. "When it says, *He guards his dear lambs with the staff of his hand,* that means he takes care of his subjects the way a shepherd takes care of his lambs. And when it says, *With a stone he shall quell the panther fell,* that means he defeats the kingdom's enemies with a small fighting force. There's no real panther or real stone."

Brennus interrupted him. "Why are we even having this conversation? Can't you see that the old man is—"

His father's warning voice broke in. "Brennus!"

"Father, I mean no disrespect. You love him because you've known him for fifty years, and you're right to do so. But even you must know that he's not sane. Let us honor the memory of the great prophet, but we can't let the ravings of a madman throw our household into turmoil."

A heavy silence followed. Aidan crept into the great hall as silently as possible, not wishing to draw attention to himself. His four brothers were huddled in the middle of the room with their backs to him. They were whispering now. His father was gazing out the window that overlooked the grape arbor. No one had noticed Aidan come in.

At the far end of the hall, by the great stone fireplace, an old man sat asleep in a chair, his arms folded, his head nodding forward against his chest. And what a head it was! White hair sprayed out in every direction; his face was buried in an enormous beard that reached down to his folded arms and sprouted out just as far to the left and right. On the floor beside him slept two goats. This must be the lunatic Brennus had spoken of.

Aidan didn't quite know what to do. He had been summoned here, yet he felt as if he were interrupting. Suddenly, the white head lurched up. The old man's big green eyes searched around the room, as if he had heard a voice and was trying to figure out where it came from. When they passed over Aidan, his eyes locked in. They seemed to see more in Aidan than any eyes had ever seen before.

The old man spoke. "Hail to the Wilderking!"

Silence. Then a little snort of laughter. Aidan heard someone say, "This is just too much." He thought the voice was Maynard's, but it was hard to say. The words sounded as if they were coming to him from underwater.

Only the old man's voice sounded clear. "Hail to the Wilderking, Corenwald's deliverer." Aidan could hear his brothers laughing. He thought they must have been laughing at him, but he didn't care. He was transfixed by the eyes of the old stranger. They shone with tears of gladness. Still the brothers laughed.

"Enough!" Father's sharp voice broke Aidan's trance. The brothers fell silent. Errol put his hand on the old man's elbow. "Come, old friend, let's sit down again."

The stranger let Errol lead him to his chair. He sat down. But his eyes never left Aidan's face.

"Aidan," said his father. "This is Bayard the Truthspeaker. You have heard me speak of him often."

"Yes, Father." Somehow Aidan already knew who the man was. He had never seen him before; indeed, no one had seen him since he left Darrow's court and took to the forest twenty years earlier. Most people assumed he was dead. And yet, when their eyes met, Aidan knew who this old man was, just as surely as the old man knew him.

Only now did Errol notice his son's disheveled state—the scratched and muddy face, the black eye, the ripped tunic.

"What happened to you, Aidan?"

Aidan looked down at himself, not sure where to begin or how much to tell.

"Whose blood is that on your tunic?"

Aidan remembered lifting the panther's body off Dobro. "That must be the panther's blood."

"Panther's blood? What panther?"

"I killed a panther, Father. With my sling. It was stalking the sheep. I slew a panther with a stone."

The room fell silent. Everyone was thinking the same thing:

With a stone he shall quell the panther fell.
Watch for the Wilderking!

"But Aidan," continued his father. "Why are you so battered and muddy? A panther slashes and bites. Does it also bruise?"

"No, Father," Aidan chuckled. "But Dobro does."

"Dobro?"

"Dobro Turtlebane. We had a wrestling match in the bottom pasture. He's one of the feechiefolk."

At this his brothers began to laugh. Now they got it; Aidan was making a joke. Wilderkings, wandering prophets, feechiefolk—it was all make-believe.

"Ha, ha! The feechiefolk! Ha, ha, ha!"

"You had me going, Aidan. I almost believed the part about the panther!"

Errol was laughing, too, as much from relief as from amusement. Then it occurred to him that if Aidan were joking, the joke was at Bayard's expense. "Be ashamed, Aidan!" he thundered. "All of you, be ashamed! It is ungenerous, it is unmanly, to tease a person who is not . . ." He had started to say "not sane" but couldn't bring himself to describe his old friend that way. "Who is not well."

Aidan was hurt that his father would accuse him of such disrespect to Corenwald's Truthspeaker. "But, Father, I wasn't teasing. About the panther or the feechie boy." Errol looked askance at his youngest son. These were wild tales indeed. And yet he had never known the boy to lie.

Bayard cleared his throat. Now that he had found what he came seeking, he was starting to carry himself more like a normal man—as if the very sight of Aidan had released him from a trance. "Oh, I don't think Aidan was teasing, old friend. I have met Dobro Turtlebane. A most unruly boy, as I remember, though not much more so than the average feechie."

Aidan's brothers could contain themselves no longer. They laughed uncontrollably and teased their little brother with the outsized imagination.

"Aidan Errolson, feechie fighter!"

"He wasn't fighting feechies; he was training them for his Wilderking army."

"From the looks of him, they should be training him!"

"Out!" Errol's voice rose above their mockery. "Leave this room!"

The brothers jostled out of the great hall, still laughing at their brother and the lunatic stranger.

When they were gone, Bayard spoke. "Errol, I should like to speak to your son. Alone. Could you leave us too?"

Errol was torn. He did not wish to disrespect the great prophet of Corenwald by refusing such a small request. But on the other hand, he had begun to believe that Bayard was out of his mind. Who knew what seeds he might plant in the boy's fertile imagination?

Errol pondered long, then answered, "Bayard, I honor and revere you as one of Corenwald's great men. You helped lay the foundation on which this nation stands." Bayard nodded appreciatively.

After a hesitation, Errol continued, "But would you now convince my son that he—and not the king you crowned yourself—is Corenwald's true king? Such thoughts are treason." It clearly pained him to speak this way to the Truthspeaker. "I cannot nurture treason in my house."

Now Bayard's eyes burned. His lips tightened. "If you revere me as you say you do," said the old prophet, "you will not suggest that I am a traitor to my king—or that I would turn your son to treachery. If I am truly a prophet of the One God, then your son is truly the

Wilderking, and you dare not hinder his progress toward that calling. But if, as you believe, I am only an old madman, I ask that you indulge me for the sake of the man I used to be."

Bayard's expression softened. "In either case, old friend, I will not make a traitor of your son. This I solemnly promise."

Errol saw the logic in the Truthspeaker's argument. This wasn't the reasoning of a lunatic. He was sorry he had offended the old prophet. Rising to leave, he put his hand on his son's head and looked into his eyes. "My son," he said, "listen well to what this man tells you."

When they were alone, Bayard turned to Aidan. "I have come to find the Wilderking of Corenwald, foretold in the ancient prophecies." He paused. "Aidan, the Wilderking is you."

Aidan stood blinking, unable to make sense of everything that had happened to him on this day. "But I'm only twelve years old."

Bayard laughed. "You didn't suppose the Wilderking would be born an adult, did you? Every great man starts out as a boy. Every great woman starts out as a girl."

"I suppose so. But I don't feel like the Wilderking."

"How is a Wilderking *supposed* to feel?" asked the prophet.

"I don't know. I don't suppose anybody knows. There's never been a Wilderking before."

"Precisely. None but you can say how a Wilderking feels. You are the only one." He poked a finger into Aidan's chest for emphasis. "And you don't have to feel anything in particular."

Bayard leaned toward Aidan. "Let me tell you a secret, Aidan." He looked over his shoulder as if making sure no one was listening, then whispered, "I don't usually feel like a prophet."

Aidan studied Bayard's face, trying to decide if the old man were joking. He seemed to be serious, but Aidan couldn't help laughing at such an absurd notion. "The great Truthspeaker not a real prophet? Now you're teasing me."

"No, no, no. I didn't say I wasn't a real prophet. I said I don't *feel* like a prophet. But my feelings have nothing to do with it. I am Corenwald's Truthspeaker because the One God shows me the truth, and I speak it."

Aidan considered what Bayard had said. "I understand. But the Wilderking will be a man of great courage. I've never shown much courage, even for a twelve-year-old."

"Today you killed a panther with a sling. Was that not an act of courage?"

"Courage? I was frightened out of my wits. You should have seen Dobro! He charged the panther like he knew no fear."

Bayard chuckled. "Oh, I'm sure of that. Most feechiefolk are fearless, especially when they are Dobro's age. But where there is no fear, there can be no courage."

Aidan was confused. "What do you mean?"

"Courage is the will to lay aside fear because your desire to do right outweighs your desire to avoid getting hurt. You said you were frightened of the panther."

"Terrified."

"Then why didn't you run away?"

Frightened though he had been, Aidan never even considered that possibility. "I couldn't leave Dobro to be eaten by a panther. I couldn't leave my sheep either."

Bayard smiled. "You felt fear. But you didn't act out of fear; you acted out of courage. Dobro was fearless. You were courageous, which is a much better thing to be."

"I was also lucky. I could try a thousand times and not hit such a perfect shot at a charging panther."

"You could try ten thousand times and not enjoy such success. But you wrong the Providence that preserves you when you credit luck for your deliverance.

"You are a skilled slinger, but neither skill nor luck explains what happened today. You succeeded for one simple reason: Long before you, or even I, were born, it was foretold that the Wilderking would slay a panther with a stone. Your act of courage fulfilled a prophecy."

For the first time Aidan began seriously to consider the possibility that Bayard was telling the truth. "What if you are correct?" he asked. "What if I am destined to be the Wilderking? How should I live?"

"The same way you should live if you weren't the Wilderking. Live the life that unfolds before you. Love goodness more than you fear evil."

Good advice, thought Aidan, but he was looking for something more specific. He was a loyal subject of King Darrow. Surely he wasn't destined to lead a rebellion against his king. He didn't quite know how to ask the question. "If I *am* the Wilderking, how do I *become* the Wilderking?"

No longer playing the role of wise teacher and adviser, Bayard had resumed the mysterious speech of a prophet.

"A traitor is no fit king. Live the life that unfolds before you. Love goodness more than you fear evil."

"Yes, of course." Aidan had more questions, but the old man was waking his goats; Aidan could see that he was preparing to leave. "Bayard, there are so many things I don't understand. The Wilderking is a wild man. He comes from the swamps and forests, not fields and pastures."

"Live the life that unfolds before you."

"Am I supposed to leave home and go live in the tanglewood?"

"Live the life that unfolds before you. You need not force yourself on the ancient prophecies."

The sleepy goats were getting to their feet. Bayard led them toward the entrance hall. "Tell your father that I cannot stay for supper. I have many things to tend to."

Aidan followed him out the front door. The old man inhaled a deep breath of spring air. "Now is the springtime. Look well to your sowing. The harvest will come in its time."

He strode down the steps, trailing his goats behind him. As Aidan watched the white ball of hair and beard bob down the cart path toward the River Road, he knew that his future was bound up with Bayard the Truthspeaker. But he still didn't know whether the old man was a prophet or a lunatic.

Chapter Six

An Alligator Hunt

Dobro Turtlebane
River Tam, below Hustingreen
Corenwald

Dear Dobro—

*I don't know how often you come to this
neighborhood. I don't even know if you can
read. But either way, I hope this letter finds you
well.*

*Things have been quiet here in the bottom
pasture since the day you were here. I've just
been doing the usual—tending sheep mostly,
helping in the fields from time to time.*

*I was hoping I'd run into you again. Maybe
you've headed back to the Feechiefen. Isn't that
where most of the feechiefolk live? Anyway,
there's something I've been wanting to ask you.
Do you know what happened to the panther we
killed? Ebbe, the servant, says he didn't see any
panther when he came down here. That doesn't*

*make any sense to me, but I never found hide
nor hair of it either.*

*Around here, everybody thinks I made the
whole thing up—about the panther, about you,
everything. Sometimes I wonder myself if I just
dreamed it all.*

*Anyway, if you find this letter and if you can
read it and if you aren't imaginary, I hope you'll
meet me here beneath this beech tree whatever
day is convenient for you. I'm usually here—
tending sheep in the afternoons, exploring the
bottomland forest in the mornings.*

*Yours very sincerely,
Aidan Errolson of Longleaf Manor*

It had been weeks since Aidan tacked the letter to the
beech tree in the bottom pasture. There it had
remained, undisturbed, ever since, as the temperate
spring yielded to the heavy heat of a Corenwald summer.
After such a promising start—a feechie boy, a panther, a
wandering prophet—Aidan's summer so far had proven
disappointing. Life at Longleaf Manor had resumed its
normal rhythms almost before Bayard was out of sight.
Aidan was back in the pasture with his sheep the day after
the prophet's visit, and there he had been most days since.

In spite of the prophet's declaration, Aidan's brothers
did not revere him as Corenwald's great deliverer. He was
still their little brother, still inclined toward make-believe,

still likely to bite off more than he could chew. For a little while, they had teased him about his interview with the crazed visitor and his claim to have wrestled a feechie boy and killed a panther. But they eventually grew tired of the joke and paid him no more attention than they had before. The fact that no one ever found any sign of the panther Aidan claimed to have killed certainly didn't help his case.

Whenever anyone asked what really happened in the bottom pasture, Aidan always stuck to his story. But even he was starting to doubt. Maybe his older brothers were right; maybe he had imagined the whole thing. The lifeless body of a full-grown panther couldn't just disappear, could it? Perhaps he only knocked the panther senseless, and it came to its senses and slinked away before Ebbe noticed it. If that were the case, Aidan hadn't slain a panther with a stone, and all this Wilderking business had nothing to do with him after all. He even began to wonder if Bayard had hypnotized him and put the whole thing in his head.

And yet he could not forget the old man's eyes—not the blank gaze that convinced his brothers that Bayard was a lunatic, but the eyes that brimmed with tears of joy when they first saw Aidan. Those were the eyes of Bayard the Truthspeaker, Corenwald's great prophet. Also, there was Father, who never dismissed any of this as foolishness. He certainly had his doubts. What sane person wouldn't? But he knew not to take any word of Bayard's lightly. He also knew that his youngest son was neither a fool nor a liar.

This was a strange and confusing time for Aidan. All his short life he had dreamed of adventure, of great deeds of heroism. Now Corenwald's Truthspeaker had looked into his eyes and told him that he, Aidan Errolson, would one day be Corenwald's greatest adventurer and hero, the Wilderking foretold in song and prophecy. But Aidan wasn't overjoyed at the news. It wasn't just that he doubted the truth of the prophet's words. The doubt, actually, was easier than belief. It was belief that burdened him with the sense—however unrealistic—that the future happiness of all of Corenwald rested on his shoulders. It was belief, not doubt, that kept him up nights.

Then there was the vague sense that even thinking about the Wilderking prophecy made him a traitor to King Darrow. He didn't ask for any of this. Even in his most ambitious flights of fancy, he had never imagined himself the king of Corenwald. His dearest hope had always been to serve the king not supplant him.

It was a lonely feeling. To whom would the Wilderking look for advice and counsel? Who could begin to understand what it was like to be headed down such a path? Not his brothers. They didn't believe any of it anyway. Father was as understanding as he could be, but his understanding was limited by his unswerving loyalty to King Darrow. Bayard was no help. He and his goats were nowhere to be found.

He couldn't explain why, but the person Aidan most wanted to talk to was Dobro, the feechie boy. He had a peculiar sense that Dobro understood him in a way that nobody else did. He thought often of the last words Dobro had said to him: "You got what it takes, that's easy to see. Even if you *are* a civilizer."

Most of his spare moments Aidan spent in the forest along the River Tam, searching for any sign of Dobro. He wandered among the meandering live oaks and spiky saw palmettos, scanning the canopy above to catch a glimpse of a lizard boy swinging from tree to tree. But he never saw anything out of the ordinary. He strained to hear the bark of the bog owl, but all he ever heard was the constant thrum of insect wings and the squawks, twirps, and chitters of the forest birds.

However, Aidan's walks in the forest served a purpose that he little realized. Every hour he spent in the Tamside Forest perfected his skills in woodsmanship. He had always known every bend in the river, every fallen log, every sandbar a half-morning's hike upstream and downstream from the bottom pasture. Now he knew every tree, every bush, every fold in the earth. He honed his climbing skills; he could clamber up all but the largest trees in the river bottom, like a natural-born feechie. He learned to tell at a glance which vines were best for swinging and which vines made the best ropes. He learned the ways of the wild boar and the bobcat.

He learned the habits of one animal in particular. An enormous bull alligator had taken possession of a little spit of sand at the river's edge near the indigo field. Every midmorning for a week, before the hottest part of the day, Aidan had seen the great reptile napping in a little sunning nest it had wallowed out in the sand. It looked to be about sixteen feet long, though Aidan had never gotten close enough to be sure.

At supper one night, he mentioned this huge alligator to his father and brothers. Father's enthusiasm was evident. "What I wouldn't give to have such a beast!" he exclaimed, rubbing his hands together.

Brennus laughed. "What on earth would you want with an old bull alligator?"

"To give it to King Darrow," Father answered, "what else?" The king kept a large game preserve on the far side of the Tam, and Errol often sent wildlife captured on Longleaf to the Royal Game Preserve, including several wild boars, a mating pair of turkeys, even an albino deer. But the alligators in the moat of Tambluff Castle were Darrow's most prized collection, and an alligator was the one animal Errol had never been able to give him. Darrow's alligators came from the southern reaches of Corenwald, near the Feechiefen Swamp. They were mostly fifteen to sixteen feet long. Alligators of that size were rare this far upriver. Errol had never found one on his estate that he considered worthy of Darrow's moat. But this one sounded like it could be just the thing.

"Next time one of those alligator hunters comes through," said Father, "we'll get him to catch that big boy for us." Longleaf Manor was the last outpost of civilization on the eastern frontier. Hunting parties heading downriver to the southern wilderness often stopped by to visit and swap news. "I don't think a sixteen-foot alligator is something I want to tangle with."

Aidan had an idea. It wasn't a very good idea. It may have been one of the worst ideas he had ever dreamed up, but he decided on the spot to carry it into execution. He would catch the alligator himself. What better way to show his loyalty to King Darrow than to single-handedly capture a bull alligator three times longer than he was tall? If he made such a gift to the king, Father couldn't possibly question his loyalty. And maybe even his own doubts on that score would be put to rest.

‡ ‡ ‡

The next morning found Aidan crouched among the leafy branches of a fallen tree that slanted down into the river. Below him, the dark water of the Tam swirled in slow eddies around the limbs that dipped and bobbed in the gentle current. By midmorning, it was already unbearably hot.

A great brown cottonmouth snake, as thick as a man's forearm, wound itself over the tree's upthrust roots and slithered down the slanting trunk toward Aidan, apparently unaware that he was there. Aidan broke off a branch with his left hand and prodded the big snake off the tree. "Sorry, friend," he said, as the snake plished into the water, "I was here first."

Aidan's right hand gripped a long wooden pole, twice the length of his shepherd's staff, with a noose of heavy hempen rope attached to the end. The other end of the rope was tied to a cypress tree near the river's edge. He was a few feet from the great alligator's sandbar.

Here Aidan had sat since sunup, waiting for his prey to approach. In the growing heat, the excitement of the hunt had slowly dissipated into numb boredom and disappointment. He expected the alligator two hours ago; soon it would be too hot for anyone—even a cold-blooded reptile—to sunbathe. He saw little point in staying much longer.

But just before Aidan gave up, the great alligator came gliding down the current and lumbered onto the gently sloped bank. It made straight for its sandy wallow and dropped down onto its belly with a snort, like a dog's. Aidan was no more than ten feet away, but he was hidden, and the big alligator hadn't noticed him.

Aidan had never been this close to such a magnificent alligator. Earlier, he had estimated it to be sixteen feet long, but he saw now that he had not given the creature enough credit. It was at least seventeen, maybe eighteen, feet from its broad, knotty head to its tree-thick tail. The great belly was as round as that of a full-grown horse.

The scars and indentions on the alligator's scaly hide told a history of many epic struggles with other bull alligators. But now it smiled the toothy, complacent smile of an animal that feared no enemy.

Aidan braced himself against a stout tree limb. He felt for his hunting horn. If he got in trouble, he could always blow it. His brothers were in nearby fields, and all of the Errolsons knew to come running anytime they heard the distress call on a hunting horn. "Let's see if you have one more battle left in you," he whispered as he lowered the noose end of the pole toward the alligator's snout.

The alligator noticed the loop descending, but it did not move. It mistook the brown rope for a cottonmouth and had no intention of surrendering this sandbar to a mere snake. When the noose touched down on the sand in front of it, the alligator hissed warningly and raised up in an aggressive posture.

This was exactly what Aidan had hoped for. With a quick flip of the pole end, he looped the noose over the alligator's snout. Only now realizing that it may be in trouble, the alligator made an explosive lunge toward the river. The lurching force tightened the noose around the big reptile's chest, just above the forelegs.

Aidan had planned to drop the pole as soon as he felt the noose tighten. But he had miscalculated the suddenness—not to mention the force—with which the alligator moved when it felt the need to. When the gigantic reptile hit the water, Aidan was still gripping the pole with both hands. The limb that supported Aidan splintered like a twig, and he catapulted out of the tree toward the snapping jaws of an angry alligator.

Chapter Seven

Home with Samson

arely clearing the alligator's gaping mouth, Aidan landed on its back, like a trick rider at a carnival. Though it didn't seem so at the moment, this was a remarkable stroke of providence. Aidan's first instinct was to jump from the beast's back and swim to safety. But it took him only a split second to realize that he had no chance of outmaneuvering an alligator in the water. He decided he was safer where he was. He scrabbled up the ridged back to a spot just behind the beast's head. He reached up under the alligator's forelegs and hugged as tightly as he could, trying to think what to do next.

When the alligator recovered from the initial shock of having a boy leap onto its back, it began to thrash back and forth with a violence that nearly shook Aidan's teeth loose. Aidan was nearly drowned with the splashing, and the bellowing roar of the furious alligator nearly deafened him. He was also taking a beating from the oaken pole, which had not broken free from the noose. But as long as he could maintain his grip, he was relatively safe. The alligator couldn't bend its head around to bite him, and its tail, though it whipped around only inches away and could knock him senseless with a single blow, didn't quite reach him.

Aidan still had no plan of escape from this predicament. He couldn't signal his brothers for help; there was no way to reach for his hunting horn without losing his grip. The alligator, however, did have a new plan. It rolled over on its back, dunking Aidan under the river. It continued rolling over and over in a sickening spin. Growing dizzy and disoriented, Aidan found it difficult to catch a breath without sucking in as much water as air. But he managed to hang on, and he was grateful not to have cracked his head on an underwater root or stump. He was also grateful that the alligator didn't roll onto its back and sink to the river mud, crushing him under its mass.

The alligator finally stopped rolling. Perhaps it was getting dizzy too. But Aidan's reprieve lasted only a few short seconds. The scaly beast carried him out toward the deep part of the river. When it had swum a few powerful strokes, it went into a steep dive. It intended to drown the boy who wouldn't get off its back.

But Aidan knew something that the alligator didn't know. The other end of the rope was still tied to the big cypress, and it couldn't pay out much farther. When he felt the rope grow taut, Aidan gathered up the last of his strength. Just as the rope jerked the alligator backward in a half-flip, Aidan propelled himself forward from the top of the alligator's head, as if from a springboard. He leaped clear, out into the middle of the river.

He had escaped—as long as the rope held. He swam out another ten strokes or so, then let the current carry him well beyond the reach of the great reptile, which was still thrashing at the end of its rope. When he was safely downstream, he swam with labored strokes back to the shallows, then waded to the sandy bank on trembling legs. He blew three blasts on his hunting horn, then lay exhausted on the bank, waiting for his brothers to arrive.

✝ ✝ ✝

The trials experienced by the Errolsons as they hauled the alligator to the riverbank, tied it up, loaded it onto a mule-drawn haycart, and drove it to the manor house compose a long and colorful story—too long to recount in detail. The whole adventure consumed a full afternoon and involved six broken ropes, the near-total destruction of a hay cart, and numerous scrapes and bruises to the Errolson brothers. Percy, who had the unenviable job of roping the thrashing tail, was flung into the river twice. The Errolsons eventually had to call on ten farm workers from the indigo field to help them heave the great beast onto the cart. No one suffered any serious harm, and no harm of any sort came to the tough old alligator.

Waiting in front of the manor house, Errol beamed with pride as he watched his sons trudge up the path. The splintered cart tilted dangerously to one side, then to the other, as the alligator hurled itself against the sides of the cart. The mules, clearly displeased, flattened their ears back against their heads. Percy halted them in the shade of a great oak tree that overhung the path.

Errol peered over the side of the wagon at the trussed and blindfolded alligator. "Just look at the great blind Samson," he laughed, as the reptile again threw itself at the wall of the cart. "He's determined to bring the walls down on himself, like Samson of old!" From that moment on, the alligator went by the name of Samson.

"Boys," Errol continued, "that's a fine animal you've caught. He'll make quite an addition to King Darrow's collection."

Aidan felt a twinge of sadness at the thought of this magnificent creature, once the master of all he surveyed, becoming part of anyone's collection, even a king's. Before this moment, he had given little thought to how the alligator might feel about things.

Errol saw the sadness in his son's face. "Aidan, you needn't worry about Samson. He'll be right at home in the moat of Tambluff Castle. Plenty to eat, plenty of smaller alligators to boss, a nice sandbar to sun himself on . . . Alligators don't ask for much more than that, do they?"

"I don't suppose so," Aidan answered, but he suspected that Samson would have preferred to be left alone.

"Yes, I'll be very proud to give such a creature to King Darrow—all the prouder because my own sons captured him." He patted Aidan's shoulder. "And I was thinking, because you boys were the ones who caught him, maybe you'd like to be the ones to deliver him to King Darrow."

The Errolsons looked at their father, then at each other, disbelieving. Was Father talking about a trip to Tambluff Castle? None of Errol's sons, not even Brennus or Maynard, had ever set foot within the castle walls. There was hardly anything they more desired to do.

"We have been invited to Darrow's castle on Midsummer's Night, two weeks hence. For a treaty feast."

A wave of excitement rippled through Errol's sons. "Which of us is invited?" Jasper asked tentatively, afraid even to hope that he might be included.

"All of us," Errol answered. "The Four and Twenty Nobles are all invited and all of their sons."

A treaty feast! The Errolsons could hardly contain their excitement. "There can be no treaty feast without a treaty," said Jasper. "Have we made a new alliance?"

A cloud passed over Errol's face. "Yes, with the Pyrthen Empire," he answered. "We have made an alliance with our bitterest enemy."

"Why do you frown?" asked Brennus. "This is wonderful news—to have our most dangerous enemy become our friend!"

"They have been fearsome foes these many years," Errol answered. "But I fear their friendship more than I fear their enmity."

"But, Father," Maynard persisted, "with the great empire as our ally, what other enemy could rise against us?"

"With Pyrth as a friend," said Errol, "we may have no need of enemies. They do not love what we love. They love only power."

He gestured at a great sprawling live oak that shaded them. "What is this, Maynard?"

Maynard thought the question odd but certainly not hard to answer. "It's an oak tree."

"You see a tree," answered Errol. "A Pyrthen sees lumber." He ran his hand along the low sweep of a massive limb. "You find beauty in such a graceful curve. A Pyrthen sees the curving ribs of the imperial navy's next warship." Samson crashed against the wagon. Errol nodded toward the sound. "You thought that was an alligator? No, that's seven pairs of officers' boots."

"Boys," he continued, "don't you ever forget how we got here. When the kingdom of Halverdy fell to the Pyrthens, your great-great-grandparents and a handful of others decided they'd rather take their chances on this uninhabited island than live under Pyrthen rule." No matter how many times he recounted this history, Errol still grew misty-eyed to think of his forebears, the last free people on a vast continent, giving up all their worldly goods and comforts to start their lives over in a teeming wilderness.

"Our very existence is an act of defiance against the Pyrthen Empire. Four times they've invaded this island. And four times the stout men of Corenwald sent them home in disgrace." Errol smiled as he thought of it. "They've swallowed up a whole continent, but people who have a taste for freedom aren't easily conquered."

Errol had spent much of his adult life fighting Pyrthens. Indeed, it seemed that all of the suffering experienced by Errol and his family had come at the hands of the great empire. He still walked with a slight limp, his leg having been crushed by a Pyrthen catapult stone ten years earlier at the fourth siege of Tambluff. Twice he had rebuilt the manor house after Pyrthen raiders had torched it in the second and third western invasions. Countless friends had died in battles with the Pyrthens. And Errol's dearest treasure—they had taken that too. His wife

Sophronia was killed in a Pyrthen raid while Errol was away at the fourth siege. Aidan was only two years old.

"Boys, you know I'm an old warrior. But I've never been a warmonger. I hope I've taught you to seek peace wherever it can be found. But an alliance with the Pyrthens . . ." Errol's voice trailed off.

"Times are changing, boys. Not everybody still keeps the old Corenwalder ways. There aren't many of the Four and Twenty Nobles who still make their sons work alongside their farmhands." He nudged Brennus, who had often voiced this very complaint. "Of the Four and Twenty, I think I'm the only one who still wears home-spun. I know things change. Still, I keep asking one question: Can Corenwald be a friend to Pyrth and still be Corenwald?"

Errol grew quiet as thoughts of the future crowded upon him. But he soon shook off his gloom. "The king knows my mind. So do the Four and Twenty, and they have decided to go forward with this alliance. There is nothing left now but to stand with them. We will speak no more of this today.

"I'll get Smithy started building a cage of iron and oak for Samson."

"From the looks of this hay cart," offered Percy, "you'd better talk to Waggoner too."

Chapter Eight

To Tambluff

On Midsummer's Eve, in the second watch of the night, Errol and his sons left on their journey to Tambluff Castle. Samson rode in his heavy iron cage on an oversize oxcart that Waggoner, the cart builder, had constructed especially for the trip. Errol and Brennus rode ahead of the oxen while Maynard, Jasper, Percy, and Aidan rode one at each corner of the cart, like a troop of bodyguards to the great alligator.

The sandy River Road shone like a white ribbon beneath the round midsummer's moon. It was easy going in the cool of the night, and there was hardly a hill all the way to Tambluff. But still they made slow progress, the team of oxen plodding along at its deliberate pace. Aidan nodded in his saddle, lulled by the rhythmic creaking of the cartwheels.

The little village of Hustingreen, two leagues from Longleaf, was still asleep when the Errolsons inched through. A small dog yapped a few sharp barks at the strangers, but he beat a hasty retreat when Samson raised his head to investigate, and they heard no more from the little dog. Aidan smiled to think of the villagers, unaware of the terrifying beast that crept only feet away from the beds where they slept so snugly.

They were more than halfway to Tambluff when the first pink rays of dawn glimmered in the east. By midmorning, they were in sight of the castle's honey-brown parapets. Tambluff Castle was situated on a high sandstone bluff overlooking the River Tam. The sandstone from which the castle was built came from just across the river and, like the bluff stone, was a rich honey color, between brown and gold. The exact match between the masonry and the surrounding bedrock gave the impression that the castle hadn't been built on the bluff but carved from it.

Tambluff Castle was nestled in a U-shaped bend where the river bulged eastward to wind around the sandstone promontory. So the castle had deep river on three sides. Along the fourth side, which bordered the city of Tambluff, the king had dug a wide moat, making an island of Tambluff Castle and providing a habitat for his alligators.

The city of Tambluff, Corenwald's capital city, sat at the foot of the castle on the west bank of the southward-flowing Tam. The city walls formed a nearly exact square mile. Three walls were perfectly straight, twenty feet high, one mile long, and built at right angles to one another. The east wall followed the river. It served as a levee to protect the city from flooding. It also protected the city from enemies who would attack from the water. Each of the walls—except the east wall, which had a moat and drawbridge—had a gatehouse in its exact center.

It was nearly noon when the Errolsons reached Tambluff's south gate. Southporter, the old keeper of the gate, recognized them from a distance and came down the gatehouse steps to meet them. "Errol, old boy," he shouted, genuinely glad to see him. "I've been watching for you. What's took you so long?" Southporter was a peasant, but he spoke to the nobleman with the easy familiarity that had long been the custom among Corenwalders of any rank.

"What's kept us, you say?" laughed Errol. "Why don't you come see for yourself?"

Walking around to see what was in the oxcart, Southporter whistled with surprise and awe. "That's quite a beast. For Darrow's moat?"

"Yes sir," answered Errol. "Aidan, my youngest son, captured him where the Tam runs along the edge of our lands."

Southporter looked at Aidan with undisguised admiration and patted him on the shoulder. "You must be some kind of hunter!"

Aidan reddened. "Father gives me more credit than I deserve. I slipped a rope around his snout, so in a way you could say I caught him. But in the end, I did no more than my brothers."

"Well, anyhow," answered Southporter, "he's a good one. King Darrow will be glad to have him."

The old gatekeeper gripped two bars of the cage and leaned over toward the unmoving alligator. He spoke to the great monster the way one speaks to a puppy in a box. "Got a name, big fellow?"

For an answer, Samson sprang to life and lunged at the gatekeeper with a terrifying roar. The clapping of his massive jaws sounded like two great planks being struck together. He seemed intent on dismembering the cheeky gatekeeper.

Southporter lurched backward and fell on the cobblestone pavement. His hat toppled from his head and rolled away. The gatekeeper quickly counted his fingers, then felt around on his face to make sure his nose was still there.

"His name's Samson," Aidan offered as he helped Southporter to his feet.

"Samson, you say? Well, Samson's manners is none too refined."

Percy chuckled. "Don't judge the poor fellow too harshly. He's had a hard day, and it's not even noon yet." Southporter looked dubiously in the alligator's direction.

"So, old friend," Errol broke in, "have the Four and Twenty all arrived?"

"I reckon so," Southporter answered, "though I can only speak to the ones what come through the south gate. Of the six of you whose estates lie south by the River Road, you're the last one to come through the gate."

"And our guests," asked Errol, "I assume they have arrived?"

The old gatekeeper's face darkened. "The Pyrthens got here three days ago. And ever since, they've been strutting around Tambluff like a passel of roosters—just like they own the place. I don't like it one bit, Errol, and I don't care who knows it."

No one quite knew what to say to this. Southporter pressed his point. "I'm just a gatekeeper, Errol. You're a great nobleman. So maybe you can help me understand. How are we all of a sudden friends with these folks?"

Errol tried to formulate an answer, but before he got a chance to speak, Southporter began again. "Four times they've brought their armies to these city walls, and four times we sent them running home like their pants was on fire. I took some pleasure in that; I don't care who knows it.

"Four times the Pyrthens' battering rams have pounded on this gate—*my* gate. My job was to pour boiling oil on their heads, but I would have gladly done it for free. I don't care who knows it."

He paused for effect. "But now we open up the west gate and invite them to traipse right in? I don't understand this, Errol!"

At the Council of the Four and Twenty a few weeks earlier, Errol had expressed these very same sentiments. He would have gladly told Southporter how heartily he agreed with him, but he held his tongue for fear of seeming disrespectful to King Darrow.

"But let me tell you this, friend," Southporter continued. "If the Pyrthens had come to the south gate instead of the west gate, they'd still be standing right where you are—outside of my wall."

Errol laughed. "Spoken like a true Corenwalder."

"A Corenwalder true and free," the gatekeeper replied. His eyes glittered with pride.

Aidan was proud to know the old man. "May you ever be so," said Errol. "But now we must be off to the castle."

"I'll send a messenger ahead of you to tell Gamekeeper Wendell that Samson is on his way."

"Thank you, friend," Errol answered. "He knows to expect us."

"He'll be mighty proud to get such a beast. And I'll be just as proud to see him go; I don't care who knows it."

Darrow's castle was only a half-mile from the south gate. But it was no small feat to maneuver the big oxcart through the narrow, crowded lanes of the capital city. Down every street, the busy throng parted before them and stared in awe at the monstrous alligator. An eighteen-foot alligator wasn't something Corenwalders saw every day, even in the big city.

Boys and girls clambered up the thatched roofs of wayside houses or hung from the signs in front of market stalls, the better to get a look at Samson. The onlookers peppered the Errolsons with questions.

"Where did you find such a monster?"

"Has he ever eaten anybody?"

"What are you going to do with him?"

A butcher leaning on the counter in front of his stall offered to buy the great reptile. "Must be a hundred and fifty pounds of meat in that tail," he remarked. But when Percy made as if to open the cage, the butcher quickly retracted his offer. He retracted his whole person, in fact, vaulting over the counter and clattering the shutters down behind him in a single, rapid motion.

Aidan and his brothers couldn't help but strut a little to see that their Samson was causing such a sensation in the city. Father, too, was visibly proud of his sons, especially of Aidan. He knew that all five had done their parts in capturing Samson. But he also knew that without Aidan's initiative and resourcefulness, none of them would have had the chance to test their strength and their wits against the great beast.

By the time the Errolsons reached Tambluff Castle, they were followed by an army of young Tambluffers—

messenger boys, shopgirls, and apprentices of all sorts who dropped what they were doing to watch the fun. But when the oxcart finally began creaking up the ramp that led to the drawbridge landing, the followers fell away. Two guards on the near side of the drawbridge signaled to two guards on the battlements above the gatehouse. The massive drawbridge began to jerk downward, a foot at a time.

The guards wore the dress uniform of Darrow's royal guard. Over a coat of chain mail hung a loosely fitting silk tunic of royal blue emblazoned with the golden boar, the emblem of the House of Darrow. The tunic was cinched with a leather belt, from which hung a scabbard and sword. The guards' round helmets were made of burnished steel and were embellished with an egret's plume dyed to match the golden boar.

As the drawbridge bumped its way down, Aidan peered over the low wall into the moat below. A tangle of large alligators wallowed and writhed over one another. But none was as big as Samson. *Father is right,* Aidan thought. *Samson will have plenty of alligators to boss.* He could see that the floor of the moat was sand rather than stone. Its gentle slope created a sandy beach where the alligators could sun themselves. There were also a number of sandbars and logs, which the larger animals had reserved for themselves. Aidan tried to guess which spot Samson would stake out when he was released into the moat.

One of the alligators in the moat snapped its jaws in Aidan's direction; Aidan flinched involuntarily. The guard standing near him smiled and winked. "Just be glad you aren't the one who has to clean that place out," he whispered.

The bridge finally dropped into place. At the far end, just inside the castle wall, waited Wendell, the royal gamekeeper. He was a red-faced, blustery man who always smelled like campfires. Aidan knew him from his many hunting trips to Longleaf.

"Welcome, welcome," he boomed. "Glad you're here. I'll take this big fellow off your hands—Samson, isn't it?—and get him ready."

Now Wendell addressed Samson directly: "You're as big as they said! Come along, now. King Darrow is going to be glad to see you. He's got big plans for you!"

And with that, Samson was wheeled away. Hostlers led the horses away to the stables, and the steward showed Errol and his sons to their apartments. There they rested until sundown, when the treaty feast was set to begin.

Chapter Nine
The Treaty Feast

The bright blast of a herald's trumpet sounded from the great hall throughout the keep of Tambluff Castle. The hour of the treaty feast had come. Across the courtyard, Aidan was admiring the new robe his father had given him for the occasion. He had never worn such finery. The bright blue cloth was thick and heavy between his thumb and finger, but soft and so smooth that it shone with a satiny sheen.

The cloth was woven from cotton grown on Longleaf Manor and dyed with indigo grown only a few feet from the spot where the Errolsons had captured Samson. But these robes were a far cry from the rough homespun cloth that the Errolsons were used to.

Errol straightened Percy's robe on his shoulders, then stepped back to admire his five sons. "Look at you," he said, half whispering. "The flower of Corenwald."

"I only wish your mother were here to see you, grown men all." Errol bit his lip and turned quickly away from them toward the door of the apartment. "The feast is beginning. We should go."

Stepping into the courtyard from the stairwell, Aidan and his brothers were astonished at the sight of what they took to be a parade of Pyrthen nobles making their way toward the great hall. They were dressed in richer clothes than the Errolsons had ever seen—richer even than the robes King Darrow wore when he visited Longleaf. The Errolsons' robes were made of the finest cotton, but the other feast-goers were dressed in silk, satin, velvet, even fur, though it was a blistering Midsummer's Day.

The courtyard was a riot of color as the evening sun glinted off the shiny satin and silken robes of red, pink, yellow, blue, green, orange, and purple. The sleeves of the noblemen's gowns were so voluminous that their richly embroidered cuffs nearly dragged the paving stones of the courtyard. Behind the great men trailed yards of extra fabric, in some cases carried by servants so it wouldn't drag. Their heavy gold chains clinked like tinker's wagons when they walked.

Their extravagant dress was downright comical. But the Errolsons soon realized that these men weren't Pyrthens at all. As they stepped into the courtyard, they began to recognize faces in the crowd: Lord Selwyn, Lord Bratumel, Lord Halbard, and his three sons. These were Corenwalders! Suddenly the Errolsons, in their close-fitting, unadorned blue robes, felt underdressed for the occasion.

"Father," called Maynard in a loud whisper. Errol was two strides ahead of them, making straight across the courtyard without looking to his left or right.

"Father, are you sure we're dressed the way we're sup-posed to be?"

Errol spun around to answer his son. He spoke through clenched teeth. "We were invited to a treaty feast not a costume party. We are dressed as Corenwalders. If our countrymen wish to preen like Pyrthens, that is their business and none of ours." He turned back and continued his march to the great hall, his step a little brisker than before.

The great hall was larger than Aidan had imagined. From end to end it was thirty-five strides of a full-grown man and from side to side twenty man-strides or more. The flames of forty torches set in the massive walls hardly provided enough light for such an enormous space, but they lent a rich glow to the honey-brown sandstone.

The ceiling vaulted up out of sight, obscured by dark-ness and torch smoke. The fireplace was piled with logs that would each require two strong men to carry, but no fire blazed on this hot, muggy night.

The walls were adorned with skillfully woven tap-estries depicting great moments in Corenwald's his-tory—Radnor's charge at Berrien, the burning of the Pyrthen fleet at Middenmarsh, the sieges of Tambluff. Interspersed between the tapestries were Darrow's hunting trophies: boars' heads, massive elk antlers, bearskins, turkey fans.

A line of seven tables placed end to end ran down the middle of the great hall. The Corenwalders, dressed in all their finery, were finding seats on the benches that ran down either side of the table. The Errolsons sat with their father near the foot of the table.

At the head of the room, beneath a massive stained-glass window, was the dais, a raised platform like a long stage running across the width of the room. On the dais sat the table of honor, one very long table made of polished walnut with carved chairs rather than benches. Two dozen wax candles on six golden candelabra provided a bright, clear light that stood in distinct contrast to the murkiness elsewhere in the hall.

All eyes turned toward the dais when a trumpet flourish rang out above the chatter of the feasters. The guests of honor, the eight members of the Pyrthen delegation, were just entering. They were led by Darrow's royal steward, a short, round man with a white beard, who showed them to their places, four seats on either side of the middle chair, which was reserved for Darrow himself.

The Pyrthens were tall and very handsome. They were dressed more or less like the Corenwalders, in silks and satins, with exquisite embroideries and embedded jewels that glistened in the candlelight. But they carried their finery with an elegance that made the Corenwalders' attempts at imitation seem all the more clownish. Earlier, Aidan had felt embarrassed for having dressed in the old Corenwalder style. Now he was glad that Father had chosen not to ape the Pyrthens' dress.

A bugler standing at the edge of the dais sounded a short tucket, and all rose to greet the entering king. Darrow looked splendid, a paragon of Corenwalder manhood. He stood over six feet tall, and even though he was close to sixty, his back was as straight as it had ever been, and his stride as sure. His royal blue robe, embroidered with the golden boar of the House of Darrow, was more ornate than the Errolsons' robes, but not nearly as extravagant as those of the Pyrthens or even the other Corenwalders. A small and simple crown sat on his graying head. His black eyes shone beneath eyebrows that were still as black as they had been in his youth. His silver beard was neatly trimmed along the square line of his jaw, and his lips, though closed, showed the slightest hint of a smile.

When the king was seated, another trumpet sounded, and the headwaiter entered the room balancing a huge haunch of roast beef on a tray. He was a short and skinny man in a white apron. He could hardly have weighed more than the enormous piece of meat he hoisted over his head. But his look of calm solemnity was undisturbed by any sign of strain as he mounted the dais steps and placed the tray in front of the king.

All eyes were on Darrow as he took a large carving knife—it looked more like a small sword—and carved eight hand-thick slices of beef, one for each of his foreign guests. The headwaiter placed a slice on each Pyrthen's plate, and Darrow stood to offer a prayer of thanks for the feast. But even as the king stood, the Pyrthens began cutting and eating their meat. Reluctant to embarrass his guests, Darrow signaled to the servants who stood in the wings, then he sat back down without speaking.

Servants began bringing in bowls and platters in what seemed to be an endless procession. The first course was a stew made of eels pulled from the River Tam, followed by smoked perch from the northern shires of Corenwald, steamed mackerel from the coast near Middenmarsh, haunches of venison, hams of wild boar, and roasted herons with their beautiful plumage still on! In between were pastries and meat pies, peaches, melons, toasted pecans, figs, and oranges brought in by the wagonload from the southernmost reaches of the island.

As the feasters were stuffing themselves, strolling lutesmen played and sang favorite Corenwalder ballads. Acrobats tumbled and wrestled and staged mock combats to the delight of the assembled onlookers. One of the entertainers juggled two live chickens while squeezing his body through a cheese hoop.

After the cheeses and wafers had been served, the court jester tootled a mock flourish on a little tinhorn and strode into the great hall balancing a huge meat pie on a tray over his head. Wearing a white apron over his green-and-yellow patchwork costume, he was a fool version of the head-waiter. With his chin lifted, his eyebrows raised above half-closed eyelids, and his mouth pulled down into a solemn frown, he mimicked the headwaiter's air of importance. But his solemnity was betrayed by his fool's cap, which flopped into his face with every step, its brass bell jingling as it bumped his nose. The feasters roared with laughter, but the jester's look of self-importance never cracked.

The assembly watched eagerly as the jester strode toward the long center table. He stumbled, and the audience gasped as the huge meat pie teetered and nearly dropped on the white head of Lord Cuthbert, the eldest of the Four and Twenty. But the jester, in an amazing feat of agility, recovered his balance and rescued both the meat pie and Lord Cuthbert.

Pacing up and down the table, the jester looked into the face of each feaster. He was seeking out the youngest member of the assembly. It appeared that he would settle

on Prince Steren, the only son of King Darrow. But then
he spotted Aidan, and he tripped his way to the far end of
the hall. In the same ceremonious way the headwaiter had
placed the beef roast in front of King Darrow, the jester
set the meat pie in front of Errol's youngest son.
Presenting Aidan with an oversized butter knife, the
jester recited a poem:

> The youngest feaster at the board
> Is just a sprout of a greater lord.
> Someday he may carve the roast on high;
> Today, the humble pigeon pie.
> Your Sovereign's dish is somewhat bigger,
> But yours, you'll find has much more vigor.
> So slice the pie, and send it round,
> That mirth and good cheer might abound.

Aidan took the big knife from the jester. He didn't
exactly follow the jester's meaning, especially the part
about his pie being more vigorous than the king's dish.
But he could see he was supposed to cut slices of the
pigeon pie as King Darrow had cut slices of the beef roast.

When the knife broke the top pastry, the pie made a
noise—a trilling coo like a pigeon. Aidan drew back in
surprise, and the gray head of a pigeon popped out of the
hole the knife had made. Two lively little bird's eyes fixed
on Aidan's face. The small round head bobbed forward
and back two times, then the pie exploded in a shower of
crumbs and bits of pastry as the pigeon burst out of the
pie and took flight, followed by a dozen more pigeons.
They whirred away in a gray blur, over Aidan's head and
out into the courtyard.

The feasters howled at Aidan's shocked expression, and at the jester's cleverness in devising a pigeon cote disguised as a pigeon pie. It took Aidan a minute to catch his breath, but when he had, he laughed as heartily as anyone in the room.

Chapter Ten

Two Speeches

As the jester capered away, King Darrow rose from his seat on the dais. The feasters' uproar died down, and the king called down the center table to Aidan, "What think you of my jester's pigeon pie, young Errolson?"

"Your Majesty, I think your jester uses the freshest meat of any chef I know."

The great hall erupted again with laughter. The king, himself laughing, remained standing. When the room was quiet enough, he began his speech.

"Dear countrymen! New Pyrthen friends! We are gathered at Tambluff Castle on an important day in Corenwald's short history. Today we join with Pyrth to say that we are no longer enemies but friends and partners; together we will build a better future."

All applauded. Darrow looked at the Pyrthen delegation on his left and right. "Pyrthens, look around you. You sit among the Four and Twenty Noblemen of Corenwald. They all have raised their hands in battle against Pyrth. Today they extend their hands in friendship."

Throughout the great hall, the Corenwalders applauded, nodding and smiling in the Pyrthens' direction. The Pyrthens, on the other hand, looked as if they might collapse from boredom. They hardly bothered to acknowledge the king's welcome. Darrow continued addressing the Pyrthens: "True, our two nations have not always seen eye to eye. But even when we faced you in battle, Corenwalders have always held the Empire of Pyrth in the highest esteem."

"Hear, hear!" said Lord Cleland, raising his goblet in salute. Lord Radnor, who sat next to a member of the Pyrthen delegation, patted his neighbor on the back. The Pyrthen shot him a dirty look and turned his back to him. At the far end of the great hall, Errol snorted; a scowl began to form on his face.

"Corenwald is still a young nation," continued the king, "a nation of explorers, of pioneers, of settlers. When we shaped a nation out of this vast wilderness, we did it alone; we had no other choice."

Swept up in the spirit of things, Lord Aethelbert raised his goblet in a toast: "To self-reliance!" Lord Halbard and Lord Cleland fixed Aethelbert with a withering glare of disapproval. Confused and embarrassed, Aethelbert withdrew his toast.

King Darrow, ignoring the interruption, continued his speech. "But we cannot remain a nation of explorers and pioneers forever. The time has come for Corenwald to settle down, to grow up, to take our place among the civilized nations of the world."

Now Lord Halbard raised his goblet and, looking in Lord Aethelbert's direction, made a toast of his own: "To the partnership of nations."

Sensing that this, and not self-reliance, was the theme of Darrow's speech, the Four and Twenty and their sons joined the toast.

"Hear, hear!"

"To partnership!"

"Hear!"

Darrow picked up where he had left off. "Corenwald has been like an old alligator: slow to move, set in its wild ways, secure in its own thick skin and in its isolation from the rest of the world. But the river of human history continues to flow. We must wade out into its current and not remain, like the alligator, mired in a stagnant swamp."

Aidan didn't like the direction this speech had taken. Darrow, keeper of alligators, was the one who had established the alligator as Corenwald's national symbol. And now the alligator had become his symbol for what is wrong with Corenwald? Aidan thought of Samson in his cage and wished he had left the poor beast alone.

"The friendship and alliance we celebrate tonight marks the beginning of a new era for Corenwald. No longer shall Corenwald be a hidebound old alligator alone in a swampy backwater. We shall be a full participant in the larger community of nations—a community that acknowledges the Pyrthen Empire as its leader."

He bowed to the Pyrthen delegation as he said this. Then he threw both arms outward in a comprehensive gesture and boomed, "Behold the new Corenwald!"

The hall shook with the cheers and applause of the Four and Twenty and their sons. But Errol was not cheering. With a stern look he made sure his sons didn't join in either. He sat as silent as a stone, his brow furrowed by a look of sadness and loss. He spoke to himself, "Alas for Corenwald."

Darrow signaled for silence. The applause gradually subsided. When the audience was quiet, he spoke again. "Before we hear from our honored guests, I want to make a presentation."

He motioned to his right, and a servant boy entered the great hall from the courtyard, leading a mule by the bridle. The mule was pulling a long, low wagon covered with a drape of blue silk richly embroidered with golden boars.

Darrow turned to the Pyrthens. "I have a gift for Emperor Mareddud. It's a bit of living sculpture that I conceived of myself. It serves as a symbol of the new Corenwald. I call it *The Wilderness Improved or Samson Gilded.*"

With a theatrical flourish, Darrow snatched away the drape to reveal a golden cage. Inside the cage was a huge golden statue of an alligator. Only it wasn't a statue. It was Samson, Aidan's alligator, and he was covered from snout to tailtip with gold paint.

Darrow had envisioned his "living sculpture" as a great golden alligator with snapping jaws and flashing eyes, roaring impressively at the assembled onlookers. It was to be a magnificent spectacle, an image of the swamp's primeval energy harnessed and improved by human art and industry. But things were not going according to Darrow's plans.

The artists who painted Samson had drugged him, feeding him chunks of meat soaked in a sleeping potion. They had no choice, really; they couldn't possibly paint an eighteen-foot alligator that was fully alert and functioning. But the effects of the potion were just wearing off when Samson was wheeled into the great hall. The poor alligator was in a stupor. His head swung listlessly from side to side. His tongue lolled out of a half-open mouth. His cloudy eyes were empty of the fiery rage that had so terrified the gatekeeper and the butcher only hours before. Once a worthy adversary for all five of Errol's sons and ten field hands, now Samson was a pitiable sight. Aidan felt ashamed for having played a part in this ugly spectacle.

A shocked gasp went up from the assembly, followed by a brief confused silence. Then a quick-thinking flatterer among the Four and Twenty started clapping. The sound of one man clapping quickly became a smattering of applause, and soon the great hall shook again with the approval of the Corenwalders. They managed to convince themselves that the gilded alligator was a clever and artistic representation of the new Corenwald, not merely a petty king's embarrassing effort to impress the emperor of Pyrth.

King Darrow basked in the applause of the nobles and made a couple of dramatic bows in the direction of the Pyrthens before returning to his seat, quite pleased with himself. The Pyrthens struggled not to laugh at the vain and silly king of Corenwald.

Errol's face reddened. Worry and sorrow were replaced by anger that King Darrow would so abuse a gift given out of loyalty and love. For the first time in his life, Errol felt real anger toward his king. He was just as angry at the Four and Twenty, the greatest men of Corenwald, now making Pyrthens of themselves, and doing a poor job of it. But the greatest portion of his anger he reserved for the Pyrthens. In their displays of friendship, they had found a surer way to destroy Corenwald than any battle plan they had ever devised.

Their enmity had always galvanized Corenwald. As pressures under the earth shape and squeeze rough carbon into diamonds, so the constant threat of the Pyrthens' tyranny had crystallized the Corenwalders' love of freedom into a hard and brilliant thing. But as impervious as the Corenwalders had been to outside pressures, they seemed to have no defense against the flattery of false friendship. Every diamond has its flaw, and as Errol watched his comrades in arms—even the high king of Corenwald—bowing and nodding to their old enemies, he realized how craftily the Pyrthens had wheedled themselves into position to crack Corenwald wide open.

When Darrow had taken his seat, one of the Pyrthens rose to make a speech on behalf of his countrymen. To the Corenwalders' surprise, it wasn't the ranking member of the Pyrthen delegation who rose, but a junior member, seated four places down on Darrow's left. He was a smirking fellow not much older than Brennus.

"King Darrow, Corenwalder friends," he began, "we thank you for your hospitality. We have found the evening to be most . . . *ahem* . . . entertaining. Like you, we have great hopes that our alliance will prove useful. Decades of fighting have been as futile for Pyrth as they have been for Corenwald. We look forward to many happy years of friendship and mutual benefit." The noblemen and their sons clapped their agreement.

The Pyrthen continued, "And as proof of our friendship and regard, I am pleased to announce that the

Pyrthen Senate has voted to cement our alliance even further. They have voted to annex Corenwald as a member state of the Pyrthen Empire."

He smiled an oily smile as the statement settled over the great hall. The Corenwalders stared at the Pyrthen diplomat, their brows knitted in confusion. They had heard this sort of language from the Pyrthens before. Four other times the Pyrthen Senate had voted to annex the island of Corenwald. And each time, the Pyrthen army had launched an invasion of Corenwald to enforce the senate's vote.

Errol sat up a little straighter. Maybe the Pyrthens would press their advantage too far. Maybe the old familiar talk of annexation would rouse the warlike spirits of the complacent noblemen and their king.

"Our previous offers to admit Corenwald into the empire have met with unfortunate hostility on your part," continued the Pyrthen. "But we are encouraged by the spirit of cooperation that has been expressed here tonight."

A buzz rose in the room as the Corenwalders began to whisper among themselves. The speaker raised his voice to be heard. "And well you should cooperate. The Four and Twenty Noblemen of Corenwald will continue to hold the lands they now hold . . . as long as they comply with the empire and its agents." The buzz began to die down.

"Should you, Corenwald's nobility, prove yourselves loyal subjects of the empire," he continued, "all the rights and privileges of Pyrthen citizenship will be extended to you and your families."

A smile of satisfaction formed on the Pyrthen's face. His audience was beginning to come around. Allowed to keep their huge estates, offered a chance at Pyrthen citizenship, the noblemen of Corenwald weren't likely to cause any trouble. And without the support of the noblemen, what trouble could the commoners cause?

The Pyrthen went on. "This island, which you have called Corenwald, will henceforth be known as the Eastern Province of the Pyrthen Empire." The buzz of whispered conversations began again.

"Oh, and there is one more thing," he continued. "In the next day or so, Pyrthen warships will land on the western coast of Corenwald . . . or, should I say, the Eastern Province. The imperial army will set up a base on the Bonifay Plain, for the defense of the empire's interests here in the Eastern Province . . . and, of course, for the protection of provincial subjects such as yourselves."

Chapter Eleven

A Hasty Council

The great hall was as silent as a tomb. King Darrow's face was blank, the pale gray of cold ashes. He slumped in his chair. He had been so focused on making friends with the Pyrthens that he had neglected the possibility that he might yet have to make war against them. Every eye in the room went from Darrow to the Pyrthen orator, then back to Darrow, looking for some sign of what to do, what to think. But the king sat motionless.

After several long seconds, the silence was broken by the crash of a heavy fist hammered once on the table at the far end of the room.

"Never!" The voice of Errol echoed around the sandstone walls. "Never! Never! Never! Never!"

Errol rose from his bench and stalked slowly toward the head table, his finger pointed at the Pyrthen diplomat who still stood there. Errol's face was scarlet, almost purple with rage. A throbbing blue vein had appeared on his forehead.

"Bring your warriors, Pyrth! Bring them by the shipload! We will leave them scattered on the battle plain, food for crows and buzzards!" The Pyrthen's confident smile melted under the heat of Errol's warlike glare. He took a step back as the tough old Corenwalder continued his slow approach.

"You are young yet, Pyrthen—too young to have sailed with the last invading army that dared set foot on Corenwald. But ask your countrymen there." Errol pointed at two Pyrthen delegates who were closer to his own age. "I daresay they remember how Corenwalders welcome invaders."

The vein in Errol's forehead was still pounding out the drumbeat of war. He continued toward the head table with slow steps. The Pyrthen, though he was already separated from Errol by the heavy walnut table, got behind his chair, in case the old man vaulted the table.

When Errol was only a few steps from the dais, Lord Radnor leaped up from his seat at the head table and put himself between Errol and the young Pyrthen. "Lord Errol," he began. His nervous grin looked more like a grimace of pain than a smile. "Let's not be hasty. No one said anything about an invasion."

"This boy just said the Pyrthens are setting up an army encampment on Corenwalder soil."

"Yes, for our protection," answered Lord Radnor with a nervous little laugh. "The treaty does state that our armies will cooperate to defend our mutual interests."

"Radnor," answered Errol with a grim chuckle, "you are not a naïve little boy! You are a nobleman of Corenwald and one of the craftiest. This is an invasion, whatever the Pyrthens say about 'protecting' us. From whom do we need to be protected if not this clutch of rattlesnakes?"

At this point, the senior member of the Pyrthen delegation stood up and supported his junior delegate by the elbow, as if he were in danger of falling over. "I think we're finished here," he announced. He turned to King Darrow. "I thank you for your hospitality."

Then he gestured toward Errol as he addressed the assembly of Corenwalders. "I hope you do not let this lunatic draw you into his madness. We have come here in friendship. Our warships come here in friendship." He hesitated, obviously aware of how ridiculous this statement sounded. "Do not court destruction at the hands of those who would be your friends."

He motioned toward the rest of the Pyrthens, and they stood to leave. Leaving through the door he entered, he called back over his shoulder, "If you need us, you can find us on the Bonifay Plain."

When the Pyrthens were gone, Errol turned and spoke to his countrymen. "From the time our ancestors first came to this island, the Pyrthens have sought to crush the dream that is Corenwald."

Radnor interrupted, "But Errol, you forget: Corenwald is not a dream. Corenwald is a kingdom. And kingdoms survive and prosper by making friends with the neighbors they cannot conquer."

Errol turned back toward Radnor. "Yes, Radnor, Corenwald is a kingdom. But first it was a dream. And the kingdom cannot stand without the dream. Our fathers dreamed of a land apart from the world Pyrth controlled. A land where power and privilege were used to serve the greater good, not to lord it over the weak. A land where even the poorest citizen could expect justice and dignity."

Radnor clasped his hands in front of him, in a gesture of earnestness. "It was a fine dream, Errol. It still is. But it doesn't change the plain fact that the Pyrthens can crush us. We all admire your courage, Errol, but we must be reasonable. The Pyrthens are hardened veterans, with the riches of a vast empire behind them; we don't even have a standing army, only untrained farmers and shop-keepers who don't know the difference between a hal-berd and a hauberk."

Radnor turned toward the rest of the assembly now, appealing to his fellow nobles' good sense. "The Pyrthens have made us a generous offer. We can join the greatest empire the world has ever seen and never shed a drop of Corenwalder blood. Or we can march out to a war we cannot win and put our homes and families in the path of devastation. There are worse things than being citizens of a great empire."

Errol's face grew red again, and the vein in his fore-head was again visible. "You astonish me," he spluttered. "For thirty-three years—in four different invasions—the Pyrthens brought the weight of a mighty empire to bear on this little kingdom. But the men and women of Corenwald proved themselves stronger even than the Pyrthens. We fought for something higher than mere conquest or the exercise of power. More to the point, something higher fought for *us.*"

Errol pushed the right sleeve of his robe up to the elbow and pointed at a long dent of a scar along the back of his forearm, a gash made by a Pyrthen battle-ax. "Many such wounds I got and gave so that Corenwald would never play the lapdog to Pyrth. Many such wounds I got and gave so we could live in a kingdom unlike other kingdoms."

He stretched his hands out toward his countrymen. "And so did each of you, the Four and Twenty of Corenwald. There's not a single coward among you." He looked into the eyes of Radnor. "Radnor, I owe my life to your acts of bravery on the fields of Berrien."

He walked toward the middle of the great hall. "Those may have been different times, but those weren't different people. That was us. You, Cleland. You, Clovis. You, Grady.

"And yet it wasn't really us. We overcame because the One God fought on our behalf—the God who asks only that we act justly, love mercy, walk humbly." He gazed out at the ridiculously ornate robes of his countrymen.

"Radnor is right; our chances of defeating the great empire are impossibly slim. But no slimmer than at any other time the Pyrthens landed on our shores.

"It has been nearly ten years since the fourth western invasion. Ten years of peace and leisure. In our comfort, we have forgotten that virtue is hard. In our wealth, we have forgotten that freedom is expensive. We have come to love what the Pyrthens love.

"So now the Pyrthens are on our shores, intent on swallowing up the nation our fathers built out of pure wilderness. And we have lost the will to drive them out. Why? Because they have offered to let the Four and Twenty keep their estates. Because we can keep living our easy lives if we cooperate with our invaders."

He pointed out the bank of windows on the south wall. "But how do you suppose Southporter, over at the south gatehouse, will feel about that arrangement? He has no great estate. All he has is Corenwald. And, by the way, he fought as hard for that dream as anyone in this room did."

He put his hand on the shoulder of one of Lord Bratumel's sons. "Or what about our sons? The next time Pyrth decides to invade some little kingdom—some little kingdom that once looked to Corenwald as a beacon of hope and freedom—they will call on our sons to do the fighting. And our great estates will seem mighty lonesome when they're gone.

"You say there are worse fates than being citizens of a great empire. But what could be worse than surrendering a dream to an enemy who was never able to take it by force?"

Errol was shaking now. His speech was finished. He seemed fifteen years older than he had looked that morning. He walked unsteadily back to his bench.

King Darrow rose to his feet. It was the first time he had moved since the young Pyrthen's speech. It seemed ages since he had last spoken, when he presented Samson to the Pyrthens. He was obviously moved by Errol's speech. He saw the futility of appeasing the Pyrthens any further. Yet the Darrow who stood on the dais wasn't the decisive leader who led the mighty men of Corenwald in four campaigns against the invading Pyrthens.

"We will meet the Pyrthen army on the Bonifay Plain." He spoke slowly. There was more resignation in Darrow's voice than resolve. The Corenwalders looked nervously at one another. "Summon the cavalry. Begin the shire-musters."

As the king spoke, the tension visibly left Errol's body. His shoulders relaxed, and his head tilted forward. At first Aidan took this change in his father's posture to be a sign of relief, even pleasure at the persuasive effect of his own speech. Aidan, too, was relieved and pleased. But his pleasure turned to horror as he watched his father slump forward onto the table, unmoving and unconscious.

Chapter Twelve

The Bog Owl
Barks Again

The Brothers Errolson
Hustingreen Regiment
Corenwalder Battle Camp
Bonifay Plain, Corenwald

Dear Brennus, Maynard, Jasper, and Percy—

*I hope this letter finds you in safety and good
health. Father and I pray for you daily, as do
Ebbe, Moira, and the rest of the servants and
farmhands.*

*You'll be happy to know that Father is doing
much better. Most of the feeling is back in his
arm and leg, and yesterday he even took a few
steps. The surgeon thinks his stroke was caused
by too much agitation the night of the treaty
feast. I'll say!*

*Anyway, the surgeon says he needs to stay in
bed, but every time I turn around, he's standing
at the western window, staring out as if he could*

*see the Bonifay Plain and look in on you from
his bedroom.*

*Please write to us soon. Please, please, please!
You've been gone two weeks, and we still
haven't heard from you. You can't imagine what
torture it is to be here on this quiet farm while
everybody else is off at war. To have no news at
all is worse than miserable.*

*Well, I hear Father stirring in the next room. I'd
better go bring him some breakfast, or he'll be up
trying to fix it for himself. You know how he is.*

Write soon. And make us all proud.

*Your devoted brother,
Aidan*

*P.S. Now that Father is almost recovered, and
because he has a houseful of servants, he doesn't
really need me here anymore. I hope he'll let me
join you at the encampment. I know I'm too
young to make a soldier, but do you think you
could get me a job as a messenger or horse boy?*

Shepherd, nursemaid . . ." Aidan mumbled to himself
as he carried Father's breakfast tray. "How do I
always get stuck with these jobs?" He put on a cheerful
face, however, as he entered Father's bedroom with a
breakfast of fruit and boiled grain.

"Good morning, Father," he said, putting the tray down on a table beside his chair. "You're up already. You look stronger every day."

"I feel stronger," Father answered. "I think I'm ready to fight some Pyrthens today. Bring me my armor."

Aidan's eyes were wide with alarm "Father! You just took your first steps yesterday. You can't—" but he saw a sly grin forming on Errol's face and realized his father was teasing. He quickly changed directions. "What I mean is, you should wait another day or two before you go to the battlefield. That way, you won't even need armor."

"Or sword and shield either," added Father. "I'll just gobble up Pyrthens, two or three at a gulp."

Father and son both laughed to think of Errol of Longleaf devouring his enemies like a dragon. But Errol's laughter broke off, and he stared out the western window. Half to himself, Errol quietly spoke: "I do hate to be laid up while the armies of Corenwald are in the field."

"Surely they can manage without you this once," offered Aidan. "Besides, you sent four warriors to the fight."

"Why have we heard no news of the battle?" Errol asked, still staring out the window. "Two weeks, and no news yet."

Aidan looked out the window, too, envisioning the Bonifay Plain beyond the western horizon. "I found Percy's favorite lantern yesterday," he said.

Errol came out of his trance and smiled at his son. For a week now, Aidan had been conjuring up excuses to visit his brothers at the battle camp. "Hmmm . . . Percy's lantern?"

"Yes. It gets dark on the plains, you know."

"Oh, indeed," answered Errol, pretending to be serious. "After the sun goes down, it gets as dark as night."

"I was just thinking, maybe I could take it to him. It's no trouble, really."

Father was laughing now. "What a generous brother! And if you're making the trip anyway, perhaps you could carry Jasper's notebook that you found the day before yesterday and Maynard's hat that you found the day before that and Brennus's pouch that you found the day before that."

Aidan frowned. "You're making fun of me. But it's hard to stay here when all my brothers are gone."

"I know it is. But there is a reason you are here and not on the Bonifay Plain: You are only twelve years old."

He tousled Aidan's hair. "You will fight one day for Corenwald—and sooner than you think. You will fight because you love Corenwald, because you love the freedom to live and worship as you see fit, because you love your family and your fellow soldiers. But you must never fight because you love the battle. You must never love the battle."

"Yes, Father," answered Aidan, a little embarrassed that he had been so eager.

An awkward silence prevailed as Errol turned his face back toward the western window. "But now I am going to surprise you," he said. He faced his son again. "Go find an empty flour sack. Fill it up with some of Ebbe's new cheeses and loaves of Moira's fresh-baked bread. Then I want you to carry that sack to the Bonifay Plain. Your brothers will be glad to get some food from home, and I will be just as glad to get any news you can bring me from the front."

Aidan's mouth dropped open with joy and astonishment. He kissed his father on both cheeks, then ran from the room to gather up his things for the trip. He was eager to get on the road before Father could change his mind.

Soon, Aidan had left Longleaf Manor and was walking north on the River Road. The sun had hardly been up two hours. On foot, it was a two-day trip from Longleaf to the Bonifay Plain—up the River Road to Tambluff, then along the Western Road from Tambluff to the plain. He couldn't ride to Bonifay. Except for a few plow mules, every horse, mule, and pony on Longleaf Manor was already there, on loan to the Corenwalder army.

He had packed light. Besides the bread and cheese for his brothers, he stuffed a clean tunic and two days' rations in the flour sack.

Aidan squinted against the glare of the summer sun reflecting off the white sand of the River Road. To his right the River Tam flowed in its black coolness. To his left, beyond the floodplain, the ancient longleaf pines towered like the pillars of God's own house, straight and smooth for eighty feet or more above the palmetto and tufting wiregrass, then opening into a deep green canopy of pine needles like green, graceful fingers. An occasional breeze brought the slightest relief from the sun's heat, as well as a piney whiff of the turpentine that oozed from the longleafs.

Just below the village of Hustingreen, Aidan rested on the white bank of Bayberry Creek where it flowed into the Tam. Leaning against the swelling buttress of a black gum tree, he remembered something Father had shown him once on the Western Road. Just east of the Bonifay

Plain was a little pond—a limestone sinkhole, actually—about thirty strides off the road. According to Father, that pond formed the headwaters of Bayberry Creek, which followed a southeasterly path to the very spot where Aidan now stood.

Aidan faced the northwest, sighting upstream along the Bayberry. If he could follow the creek to its source, he would come out on the Western Road, only a league or two from his destination. It wouldn't be easy going, for there was no road that way, but surely the shortcut would save him at least four or five leagues. And besides, in the shady creek bottom he could avoid the direct sun of the open road.

He decided to try it. He left the River Road and made for the tanglewood. The bottomland forest quickly enveloped Aidan in its twisting branches and trailing vines. The trails he followed were not made by people, but by deer and bear and wild boar. In places there weren't even animal trails, and Aidan had to make his own.

The sun filtering through the dense treetops cast a greenish light on Aidan's surroundings. The shade of the big gum trees and water oaks took the edge off the heat, but still Aidan's tunic was soaked through with sweat, for the air was heavy and damp in the creek bottom.

Insects were the one thing Aidan had failed to consider when he quit the road and took to the deer paths. In the swampy bottoms, the bugs multiplied like a plague of Pharaoh. Aidan trudged along in a humming cloud of mosquitoes, slapping, swatting, and waving his arms to fend off their attacks. The gray sweat bees, though much less numerous than the mosquitoes, tormented him. Their big sting was out of proportion to their tiny size.

But no sound in the forest was more immediately terrifying than the whining buzz of the yellow flies. They came in hard and fast, flying an erratic spiral that made them impossible to swat. They were so fierce and persistent that they didn't even need bare skin to sting. They thought nothing of landing on Aidan's thick hair and boring straight through to his scalp. A couple even pierced through Aidan's tunic, raising angry red welts on his shoulder. These were the sort of bugs that one seldom met on the big road. They were known only to the adventurous soul who left the well-worn path to explore the swamps and river bottoms.

But Aidan's shortcut also revealed to him many wondrous things that he could have never seen on the road. Every bend in the creek brought some new delight: a pair of otters cavorting in the water, a parade of wild hogs snortling and rattling through the saw palms, a regiment of turtles lined up side by side along a fallen log. The woods were dense and tangled, but Aidan was in little danger of losing his way. He had only to keep near the creek and continue upstream, and he would eventually reach the lime sink at the head of the creek.

After two hours' hike upstream, however, things got more complicated. The creek spilled into a broad swamp. Only now did it occur to Aidan why there was no road through this part of the country. The sandy track that he had been following deposited him on a smelly mud flat, and he sank to his ankles in hot mud. He strained to free his feet, and the muck made a loud sucking sound, then a pop as each foot came loose. Watching his footprints slowly fill with oily, putrid water, Aidan mulled over his dilemma. He no longer had the convenient option of trekking up the creek bank, for there was no more creek bank, only a sunken morass of deep, sticky mud punctuated by a maze of rivulets and a few stunted cypress trees. Unless he wanted to swim up the creek, his only choice was to turn north and circle around the swamp along the sand hills and meet back up with Bayberry Creek wherever he could. Not knowing how big the swamp was, he didn't know how much time he would lose on this detour. But he had little choice.

Coming out of the creek bottom, Aidan found easier traveling among the sparse pines of the sand hills. But it was past midday, and the sun glaring on the sand was a stark contrast to the shady green of the creekside. Aidan sought shade in a stand of big magnolia trees.

He closed his eyes and leaned his head back against the smooth, gray bark of a big magnolia. Just as he began to doze, he heard a rattle in the stiff, waxy leaves overhead. And yet there had been no breeze to rustle in the treetop. He stood and craned his neck to peer into the branches above. He sniffed the air. Was that pungent, fishy smell wafting up from the swamp or down from the tree? He circled around the tree, ducking beneath its low limbs. The deep green leaves were thick, but he could see movement of some sort in the highest branches. Something up there—or someone—was circling the trunk opposite him, keeping itself hidden.

Then Aidan heard a sound he had been waiting all summer to hear: *Ha-ha-ha-hrawffff-wooooooooooo . . . Ha-ha-ha-hrawffff-wooooooooooo.*

The bark of the bog owl! It thrilled Aidan just as it did the last time he heard it in the bottom pasture. He threw back his head and answered as best he could: *"Ha-ha-ha-hrawffff-woooooooooo."* Then he belted out the battle cry that Dobro had sung when he took off after the panther: *"Haaaawwweeeeeee!"*

Aidan mounted a low limb of the magnolia and started scrambling up, overjoyed to find the friend he had been seeking all summer long. "Dobro!" he shouted. "Dobro! Dobro! You stinking mudfish! I've been looking all over for you!"

He was halfway up the tree when another call echoed from a few feet away in another magnolia: *Ha-ha-ha-hrawffff-woooooooooo . . . Ha-ha-ha-hrawffff-woooooooooo.* He turned toward the second call, then he heard a swift rustle coming down the trunk of his tree. He jerked back around, just in time to glimpse the soles of two flat, gray, hairy feet flying toward him. Aidan's chest caught the full force of the blow, which propelled him out of the tree. When his head hit the sandy ground below, Aidan's world went black.

Chapter Thirteen
A Trial

When Aidan woke up, his head was throbbing and he couldn't see. He was on his back, facing skyward—at least, he thought he was. At the same time he felt as if he were moving. His wrists and ankles ached. The air was so stuffy he could hardly breathe, and his mouth was tight and stretched. His parched tongue felt furry in his mouth.

Aidan's senses were returning slowly. He was confused and found it difficult to figure out where he was. It occurred to him that he had been hearing a steady splashing, as well as voices, one near his head and one near his feet. As the fog cleared, the words he heard began to make some sense.

"You don't reckon you kilt him, do you?" asked the voice near his head. It was a high-pitched, grating voice.

"Course not, Rabbo," said a nasally voice near his feet. "He'll be all right . . . for a little while, anyway."

Both voices laughed. Aidan didn't get the joke and wasn't sure he wanted to. A sudden jolt shook his whole body, and a new ache shot through his wrists and ankles.

At his head he heard a shrill laugh from the voice called Rabbo. "Watch out for that cypress knee, Jonko. The prisoner might not appreciate you dropping him in the swamp."

"Shut your feeder, Rabbo."

"You shut your own feeder."

"How 'bout you make me?"

"How 'bout I take this tote-pole and learn you some manners?"

"Awwww, dry up, Rabbo. We'll be at the Meeting Hummock in no time. I'll settle up with you there, where the whole tribe can watch the whupping."

Aidan was beginning to put the pieces together. Two men named Rabbo and Jonko—feechiefolk, by Aidan's estimation—were carrying him on a pole between them, the way hunters carry a stag or a boar. His wrists and ankles were tightly bound; they bore his weight as he hung face-upward. His kidnappers had put a heavy bag over his head, probably made from an animal skin, from the smell of it; that explained why it was so dark and why it was so difficult to breathe. He couldn't cry out because they had gagged him with vines. The fuzzy sensation on his tongue was a leaf from the vine gag.

Jonko, who held the end of the pole near Aidan's feet, was leading the way. They were slogging through a swamp on their way to a place they called the Meeting Hummock. But what sort of things happened at the

Meeting Hummock? Aidan's stomach tightened as he imagined the possibilities.

Before long the splashing stopped, and Aidan heard instead the tramp of his captors' feet on dry land. They were on an island—the Meeting Hummock? Rabbo and Jonko were no longer on speaking terms, so Aidan could glean no more from them. But in the near distance he heard a feechie call, *"Haaawwwweeee,"* and Jonko's answer, *"Haaawwweeee."* They were coming up on at least one feechie, maybe more than that.

As Jonko and Rabbo continued on their way, Aidan heard a buzz of voices in the near distance. The farther they went, the louder and more distinct the voices grew. But just as they drew close enough that Aidan could make out a few words, and even a whole sentence or two, the conversation abruptly broke off. Aidan pictured a crowd of feechiefolk watching in silence as he was carried in like a hunting trophy.

Aidan could feel himself being lowered to the ground. The tote-pole was pulled away, though his wrists and ankles were still bound. A voice at his ear, Rabbo's, he thought, whispered, "On your feet, young civilizer," and he felt a hand grab his wrist and pull him up to a standing position.

Someone removed the hood that had hidden Aidan's face. He stood blinking in the afternoon sun; the glare made his aching head pound even harder. When his eyes focused he could see he was standing at the center of a semicircle of feechiefolk. There were at least a hundred of them. Their pinched, gray faces were contorted in various attitudes of curiosity, hostility, and fear. Some fixed

Aidan with threatening stares, baring what few teeth they had like mean dogs. The wee-feechies covered their faces with their hands and peeked out at Aidan between their fingers. Most of the tribesmen, though, gaped open-mouthed at the strange creature brought to their Meeting Hummock. Those in the back craned their necks for a better view or tried to push toward the front row. All their lives they had heard about civilizers; even the tiniest wee-feechies knew to fear them. But except for the scouts and the elders, most of them had never actually seen one.

The feechies were small people. The full-grown he-feechies were barely taller than Aidan, though their turtle-shell helmets added a couple of inches to their height. They were all lean and sinewy, even the youngest wee-feechies. They all had the same gray skin as Dobro. Their hair was thick and coarse, of various colors, but they all had roughly the same haircut: short and jagged across the front, longer in the back, and lumpy all over.

Most of the feechies wore reptile skins. The adult he-feechies went bare-chested and wore snakeskin kilts and turtle-shell helmets. She-feechies and youths of both sexes wore tunics fashioned from alligator skins. Wee-feechies wore little loincloths made from possum or muskrat hides. All were barefoot.

Many of the feechiefolk wore various other adornments that betokened their hunting skill: bear-claw neck-laces, egret-plume headdresses, boar-tusk bracelets. A few wore capes made from wolf hides or bobcat skins. One youth in the front row appeared to be wearing a panther hide. He was a surly fellow who never even raised his head to look at Aidan.

For several seconds, Aidan and the feechiefolk stared at one another without speaking a word. Two he-feechies stood beside him, one holding each elbow. They were Jonko and Rabbo, Aidan's captors, and he was glad to have them, for it is no easy matter to stand with bound ankles.

An elderly feechie came out of the crowd and walked toward Aidan. He was a bent and toothless old thing, but many years' rough wisdom shone from his one good eye. He was Gergo Snagroot, chieftain of this band of feechies. He looked Aidan over from head to toe and back up again, then turned to address the assembled feechies.

He pointed at Aidan. "In case some of you didn't know it already, this here is a civilizer."

One of the wee-feechies, her eyes wide with terror, bolted away and ran screaming into the woods. The other wee-feechies weren't quite so terrified, but they were confused. They had been under the impression that civilizers—if such things even existed—were some sort of monster. But this so-called civilizer didn't look all that different from a feechie, only a little paler and softer, and dressed funny.

"Ain't he kind of little for a civilizer?" asked a squint-eyed she-feechie in the third row.

"He ain't got its full growth yet, but he's a civilizer, all right," answered Chief Gergo. "And we got to figure out what to do with him."

"Boil him," someone suggested.

"Drown him," offered a young feechie in a beaver-skin cap.

"Throw him out of a pine tree."

"Feed him to a alligator."

The crowd was growing more enthusiastic as they warmed to their subject. Aidan suspected that the only thing keeping the mob from doing him some awful violence was the fact that they couldn't agree on which awful violence to do.

At last Chief Gergo raised a three-fingered hand to silence the crowd. "Hold on, hold on, hold on!" he squeaked. "We ain't doing anything to this civilizer until I say what we're doing to him. And I ain't saying until we've had some more confabulation."

He turned toward Rabbo and Jonko. "Jonko Backwater and Rabbo Flatbottom is the ones what caught him. And I reckon they ought to tell us how it happened."

"Well," began Rabbo, "me and Jonko got a hankering for some gopher, so we was ranging around on the sand hills. Jonko's poking around in a gopher hole, and I'm looking for another one, when I see this little civilizer coming out of the creek bottom, making straight for us."

"There ain't no civilizer road around them sand hills," interrupted one of the feechies in the crowd.

"That's what I know, Verno. That's why we was so surprised. Anyway, I give Jonko the skeedaddle signal, and we make for a jumble of magnolia trees and scoot up."

"We didn't want no civilizer trouble," explained Jonko.

"Well, the civilizer starts trooping up the sand hill," continued Rabbo, "and where do you reckon he decides to flop down and rest?"

"By *my* magnolia tree, that's where!" answered Jonko. "I stayed as still as I could, but magnolia leaves is so rattlesome, can't nobody keep quiet in a magnolia tree. I reckon the civilizer heard me, 'cause he starts doing everything he can to see what's in the treetop." Jonko mimicked the way Aidan circled and ducked and craned to get a glimpse of him.

"I could see that hiding wasn't working out," Jonko continued. "So I decided I'd scare him off."

Rabbo laughed as he remembered. "Jonko cut loose with the loudest, scariest watch-out bark I ever heard." He threw back his head in imitation: "*Ha-ha-ha-hrawffff-wooooooooo . . . Ha-ha-ha-hrawffff-wooooooooo.* There ain't never been a civilizer wouldn't run home crying when he heard something like that."

"Except this one," said Jonko, pointing a thumb at Aidan. "He answers back with a watch-out bark of his own."

Rabbo was getting more excited as he relived the scene. "Then he cuts loose with a feechie battle yell!"

"A battle yell!" exclaimed Chief Gergo. "How would a little civilizer know the feechie battle yell?"

"I don't know, Chief," answered Jonko, "but Rabbo and me both heard it."

Aidan would be glad to tell them everything if only they would untie the vine gag, which was making his jaws ache. He would tell them all about Dobro and their encounter in the bottom pasture. But none of the feechies seemed interested in what Aidan had to say. Everyone just eyed him quizzically. Everyone except for the young feechie in the panther cape. He only pulled the hood down farther over his face.

"You not going to believe what happened next," Jonko continued. "This civilizer starts climbing the tree like he wants to get at me."

"When I seen that," said Rabbo, "I give a watch-out bark of my own. And when the civilizer turned in my direction, Jonko swung down and give him a whole mouthful of feechie foot."

"He done the prettiest back-over flip you ever seen," said Jonko. "He was still knocked out when we tied him up and carried him off on the pole. We gagged him with vines so he couldn't holler for more civilizers, though I don't reckon there would be any civilizers to holler for, this far off the road."

Chief Gergo whistled. "Sounds like you was just defending yourselves. It also sounds like you wasn't the first feechiefolks this civilizer had ever seen. Anything else he said or did before you knocked him out?"

"Well," Jonko began, "he did say something, but I couldn't make no sense out of it. I don't speak civilizer talk."

"What was it, then?" pressed Gergo.

"When he was climbing up the tree, he kept hollering, 'Dodo,' and I think he said something about looking for a mudfish."

"Naw, that ain't it," interrupted Rabbo. "He didn't say nothing about no dodo. It sounded more like 'Toe Gro!'"

Jonko was irritated. "I know what I heard, Rabbo. He was saying, 'Toad Row.'"

Rabbo put his hands on his hips and sneered at Jonko. "That don't make no kind of sense, Jonko. He was saying, 'Go, Foe.' No doubt about it." The two feechies were chest to chest now, each ready to fight for his own misinterpretation of what Aidan had said. *If they would only unbind me and let me speak for myself, I would happily clear things up,* Aidan thought. He could tell them that he wasn't saying "Dodo" or "Go Foe" and certainly not "Toad Row" but "Dobro."

There was another person in the crowd who could have guessed what Aidan was saying when he climbed the magnolia tree: the boy in the panther cape, who now was hiding his face completely. He was Dobro Turtlebane, and he was terrified of what might happen next . . . to himself, to Aidan, or to both of them.

Rabbo and Jonko were now dancing circles around each other, glaring and raising their fists.

"I'm gonna jump down your throat and stomp your gizzard!" Rabbo threatened.

"I wish you'd try," answered Jonko. "It's nothing to me to swallow a man whole."

Feechies love few things better than a fistfight. The prospect of Rabbo and Jonko coming to blows made them forget completely about the defenseless civilizer who stood between them, gagged and bound hand and foot. The whole mob pressed closer to get a better look at the two combatants—everyone except Dobro. He moved against the pulsing tide of feechiefolk, trying to get to the back of the crowd where he would be less conspicuous.

But it was hard to be inconspicuous in the press of a crowd. Trying to pick a hole to push through, he stood right in front of Odo Watersnake. "Move it, Dobro!" shouted Odo. "I can't see!"

In his haste to get out of Odo's way, Dobro stepped squarely on Theto Elbogator's bare foot. "Yow, Dobro!" Theto yelled, and he pushed him into Benno Frogger.

"Stop it, Dobro!" yelped Benno, giving Dobro a push that sent him sprawling into the middle of the crowd, the tail of his panther cape flying behind him. He bowled over four she-feechies and three wee-feechies. Everyone's attention shifted from Jonko and Rabbo to Dobro. "Dobro!" the crowd scolded, as if with a single voice.

Jonko and Rabbo dropped their fists and stared, first at one another, then at Dobro. "Dobro!" they both shouted.

The crowd looked back at them. "That's what the civilizer was saying," Jonko nearly shouted, pointing excitedly at Dobro. "He was saying, 'Dobro! Dobro! Dobro!'"

Chapter Fourteen

A Verdict

Someone pushed Dobro from behind, and he stumbled into the open space where Jonko, Rabbo, and Aidan were standing. A she-feechie was right behind him. She looked exactly like Dobro—an older, female version of Dobro. She was his mother, Luku Turtlebane. "Dobro!" her shrill voice silenced the noise of the crowd. "Dobro Turtlebane! How come this civilizer knows your name?"

Dobro stood frozen, not sure what to do or say.

Mrs. Turtlebane grabbed Dobro's ear and began to twist it. "All right, all right, all right," Dobro squealed, pulling loose from his mother's grip. "I know this civilizer. His name's Aidan of the Tam." He paused and rubbed his sore ear. "Yeah, I know him, and I ain't sorry about it neither."

"What you mean, boy?" demanded Dobro's mother. She made another grab for his ear, but he eluded her. "You better explain yourself."

"This civilizer saved my life."

A gasp went up from the crowd. Mrs. Turtlebane's hands were on her hips. "Saved your life from what, boy?"

"From a panther." He gestured toward the panther hide he wore for a cape. "From this here panther."

"You told me you kilt that panther your own self."

Dobro looked down at his feet. "Mama, that ain't the truest tale I ever told." He looked over at Aidan as he remembered what happened. "I was getting chased by this panther—and he was bearing down on me pretty good—when Aidan kilt him with a rock."

"A rock?" snorted Rabbo. "You can't kill a panther with a rock."

"Aidan can," answered Dobro, smiling toward his civilizer friend. "He's got a rock slinger. He's pretty handy with it too."

Mrs. Turtlebane stared at Dobro, trying to decide how much of his story to believe. Then she stared at Aidan and back at Dobro. Finally, she took a deep breath, squared her shoulders, and raised her chin in a posture of firmness. The crowd grew perfectly quiet as Mrs. Turtlebane stalked toward Aidan. Her eyes were fierce with a mother's protective instincts.

Aidan was terrified. His hands and feet were still bound, so he could neither run away nor defend himself. And gagged as he was, he couldn't even beg for mercy. He steeled himself to receive whatever punishment this fierce she-feechie had in mind for the civilizer who had corrupted her son.

Dobro's mother stood directly in front of Aidan, that strange light still in her eyes. Looking intently at the civilizer, she reached her right hand toward Rabbo. "Give me your knife, Rabbo."

Rabbo hesitated. He didn't want to see the civilizer killed without a proper trial. But Mrs. Turtlebane kept her hand outstretched. The intensity of her mother-love finally bent Rabbo's will to her own, and he handed over the stone knife.

Mrs. Turtlebane pointed the blade in Aidan's face, three inches from his chin. Aidan did his best to breathe evenly and not to whimper; he was the only civilizer these people had ever seen, and he didn't want to give the impression that civilizers were a tribe of whiners or cowards. "I don't want no civilizers around my boy," she said, sneering at the prisoner.

Mrs. Turtlebane made a quick upward thrust with the stone knife. Aidan closed his eyes and offered up a quick prayer, sorrowful that his life was ending so early and so suddenly. He felt no pain. But on the other hand, he didn't feel dead either. Opening one eye, he saw the vine gag lying on the ground, cut in two. Opening the other, he stared at the she-feechie sawing away at the vines that bound his hands.

"I don't want no civilizers around my boy!" Mrs. Turtlebane repeated. Then she broke into a greenish grin. "But for them what saves his life, I can make an exception."

She went to work on the vines that bound his feet. When she had gotten him free, Mrs. Turtlebane fell on Aidan with a hug so fierce it nearly squeezed the breath out of him.

The terrible she-feechie was now sobbing. "Hawww, hawww, hawww! You saved my Dobro. Hawwww, hawww, hawww. Bless your head and liver. Hawww, hawww, hawww. You rescued my sweet Maypop from that bad old panther." She planted kisses on both of Aidan's cheeks, two on his forehead, and one on top of his head just to make sure. Aidan shrank from her prickly chin whiskers and her fishy breath, but he had to admit that this situation had greatly improved in a few short minutes.

But Aidan's ordeal was far from over, as he realized when Chief Gergo stepped forth again. The old feechie chief was ready to pronounce his verdict on the prisoner.

"The feechiefolks only got one defense against the civilizers, and it's this: The civilizers don't believe we exist. If they did, they would civilize us right off of this island."

"You said something there," came a voice from the crowd.

"Down with civilizers," shouted a second voice.

"Feechies forever!" whooped a third.

Ignoring the crowd, Gergo pressed on. "That's why the feechie code says that no civilizer can see a feechie and live. Dobro Turtlebane, when you showed yourself to this civilizer, you put a death sentence on his head." Aidan turned pale. Cheers rose up from some of the feechies in the mob.

"Let's roast him!" suggested someone in the crowd.

"Feed him to the fire ants," offered another.

Aidan felt the breath go out of him. Mrs. Turtlebane clutched Aidan tighter in her protective arms. Dobro was sobbing now.

"But," said Gergo. "*But*," he repeated more loudly, silencing the unruly crowd, "there's another law in the feechie code. It says that nobody who saves a feechie's life should die by a feechie's hand. That's one law I don't aim to break today. Aidan, you gonna live." Aidan's knees felt weak from relief.

"And what's more," continued the feechie chief, "as the chieftain of this band of feechies, I declare Aidan of the Tam to be a feechiefriend, for the gumption he showed rescuing Dobro Turtlebane from a panther. Tonight, we'll have a feechie feast to make it official."

The crowd erupted in loud hoots and barks of approval. Aidan wasn't sure if they were cheering because his life had been spared, or if they were only happy at the news of a feechie feast. Some of the feechies hooting the loudest now were the same ones cheering when it looked as if he would be put to death. It would be a long time yet before Aidan really understood anything about the feechiefolk.

Chapter Fifteen

A Fishing Trip

The feechies scattered to make ready for that night's feast. Some went to collect berries and fruit, others in search of roots and grubs. Fishing parties were hastily organized and dispatched to the choicest fishing holes in the swamp. The wee-feechies dispersed to gather forest flowers with which to decorate the Meeting Hummock.

Soon only Aidan and Dobro remained in the meeting spot. Dobro wasn't the same brash, blustering fellow Aidan had first met in the bottom pasture. Aidan could tell he was struggling for words. At last Dobro spoke. "Aidan, I never meant to cause you no trouble."

Aidan smiled at his feechie friend. "Maybe a little trouble is just the thing I need, Dobro," he answered. "Civilizer life can get pretty boring. On the other hand, getting boiled or roasted or fed to alligators—that might be a little more trouble than anybody needs. I'm mighty glad you were here to get me out of that mess."

"I didn't do right, Aidan."

"What are you talking about? You saved my life!"

"That may be, but my first thought was to run away from a whupping. What you reckon would have happened to you if I really had run away?"

"You wouldn't have really run away."

"How do you know that?" asked Dobro.

"You got what it takes, Dobro," said Aidan, grinning. "Even if you are a feechie."

For the first time since Aidan had arrived at the Meeting Hummock, a smile covered Dobro's face. He clamped Aidan in a headlock and flipped him into a mayhaw tree, just to show how much he appreciated his kind words.

"Say," said Dobro, as he helped Aidan back down, "how 'bout we find one of them fishing parties? I believe some fishing would do me good."

Aidan agreed, and the two boys headed for the main creek bed. The dry ground of the hummock soon ran out, and Aidan found himself slogging through the very swamp he was trying to avoid when he first fell in with Jonko and Rabbo. Soon the sound of exuberant whooping echoed through the cypress trees.

"Sounds like Doyno and Branko," said Dobro, slowing down to listen. "They must be over at Mussel Bend. They're the best fishermen you ever gonna meet. If there's a catfish left in that creek, Doyno and Branko can find him."

Dobro quickened his pace, energized by the whooping of the fishermen. "Are they going to have enough poles for us?" asked Aidan.

"What kind of poles?"

"Fishing poles."

"Naw, naw, naw. This is serious fishing. We ain't got time for fishing poles—not when it's nearbout time for the feast already."

Aidan's curiosity was aroused. What sort of fishing would be more serious than pole fishing?

"There they are!" announced Dobro pointing through the trees where the main channel ran. Aidan saw only one person where Dobro was pointing, a feechie youth about his age standing in water up to his chest. Suddenly, the water beside him exploded in a huge splash, and a second person emerged, holding a big gray catfish that reached halfway to his shoulder. Doyno and Branko resumed their victorious whooping.

"Where did that catfish come from?" Aidan asked, his mouth open with wonderment.

"He grabbled it."

"He did what?"

"He grabbled it. He caught it with his hands."

Aidan gave Dobro a sidelong look. Dobro explained. "Nearbout every stump, every fallen log, every abandoned muskrat hole in this swamp got a big catfish hiding in it or under it. And that catfish believes he's the true and rightful owner of that spot. Any other fish—redbelly, bluegill, punkin seed, pike, bigmouth, bugle mouth, warmouth, garfish, jackfish, mudfish, shad, eel, anybody but a catfish—you come poking around their hole, they scoot off in a hurry." He waggled his hand to simulate a fish's hasty retreat. "But not Old Whiskers. He'd rather fight you. So when you wiggle your fingers in front of his face, he's sure to grab aholt of you. Then you pull him out. Only he's going to be trying to pull you in."

Aidan stared in disbelief. "Have you ever done it?"

"Sure," answered Dobro. "All the time." He showed Aidan his forearm, scarred from the rasping jaws of many catfish.

"Doesn't it hurt?" asked Aidan.

Dobro thought for a second. "Yeah," he said with a chuckle, "I reckon it does."

Another loud splash drew away Aidan's attention. Branko had gone underwater. Half a minute later he broke the water's surface again. In his right hand he gripped not another catfish but a cottonmouth snake. Its terrible white mouth was open so wide that it seemed to be folded inside out. The snake twisted and writhed, struggling to find something to sink its fangs into. *"Haaawwwweeee!"* whooped Branko.

"That's another thing," Dobro pointed out. "Sometimes them holes and stumps got cottonmouths. Snapping turtles too. That's something you got to watch out for."

Branko held the huge cottonmouth out where Doyno could get a good look at it. Then, to Aidan's horror, Branko heaved the deadly snake onto his fishing partner. Doyno caught the snake like a hot potato and slung it into the woods in a single motion. Branko howled, laughing at his own joke. Doyno didn't think it so funny to have a venomous snake thrown on him.

"You trying to kill me?" Doyno bellowed. "Put 'em up, Branko. I aim to feel your short ribs."

Doyno shinned up a nearby cypress tree and dove down onto Branko's back. The opponents whirled and splashed like a waterspout, lost to sight in a cascade of creek water. Dobro and Aidan jumped into the water and waded across to the place of combat.

"Hold on there, boys," said Dobro, raising his voice above the noise of the battle. Branko and Doyno stopped where they were, surprised to hear another voice. Doyno was holding Branko by the hair, about to dunk him under the water. "I hate to bust up your little frolic," Dobro continued, "but I got somebody here ain't never grabbled for catfish and wants to give it a try."

Aidan gave a start. He wanted to do no such thing. "Oh, I don't know," he began. "I don't think that'll be—"

"Of course, sure, sure," said Doyno, releasing Branko and wiping his hands on his tunic. "I know just the spot for a first-timer."

He led Aidan and Dobro across to a fallen tree, the roots of which jutted out of the water. "They's usually a big one lurking up in there," he said, pointing to the tangle of roots. "Every time I pull one out, next day one just as big has took his place. Just poke around in there. You'll find one."

Aidan sidled over to the root tangle and pretended to feel around underwater. But his heart wasn't in it. He had no desire to get bitten by a big catfish, and he certainly had no desire to get bitten by a snapping turtle or a cotton-mouth.

"Naw, naw, naw," coached Doyno. "You won't never catch him that-a-way. You got to reach way down yonder. If you ain't ducking all the way under, you ain't reaching down deep enough."

Doyno, it seemed, genuinely wanted Aidan to succeed. "Here," he said, "I'll go down there with you and show you where to look."

Doyno dove underwater, and Aidan saw no choice but to go after him. In the murky water, he could see very little besides light and shadow and movement. But he could see enough to tell that Doyno was pointing with animated jabs toward a shadowy spot near the creek's sandy floor. Aidan halfheartedly stuck his hand in the gap where Doyno was directing. He didn't wish to disappoint Doyno, but on the other hand, he wouldn't try any harder than he had to.

Aidan had hardly gotten his hand in the hole when two bony jaws clamped down on his wrist. His hand was in the slimy innards of a creature big enough to swallow his hand whole! His first reaction was to snatch his hand away. But the creature wasn't letting go. Aidan pulled and strained, but the jaws only tightened on his wrist. As the struggle continued, Aidan could feel himself getting dizzy; he had blown out all his air in the initial shock, and he was getting desperate for a breath. He willed himself to make one last tug, and he pulled loose.

When Aidan broke the surface of the water, his attacker was still latched onto his arm. It was the biggest catfish he had ever seen—a brownish, spotted monster with dull bluish eyes and whiskers as big around as Aidan's little finger. The fish was as long as Branko's cottonmouth and nearly as big around as Branko himself.

"*Haawwweeee!*" whooped the feechies exultantly.

"I ain't never seen a first-timer do that!" yelled Doyno. "This here civilizer's got what it takes!" He was thrilled with his student's success and secretly felt that he deserved at least some of the credit himself.

Aidan thought they were giving him too much credit. It was the catfish, after all, that had caught him, not the other way around. Nevertheless, the four fishermen, three feechies and a civilizer, marched their catch triumphantly to the Meeting Hummock, where the festivities were just getting started.

Chapter Sixteen

Another Feast

The feasters marveled at Aidan's catfish, and they all congratulated him for his skill and bravery. The cooks, who were beginning to doubt they would have enough fish for a proper feast, were especially grateful to have such a large quantity added to their store.

Unlike the treaty feast at Tambluff Castle, there was very little pomp and ceremony at the feechie feast. The feechies wore the same clothes they had worn earlier in the day. They sat where they pleased, or stood, if that's what pleased them, for there were no tables anyway. There was no trumpeting or standing up or sitting down when Chief Gergo showed up. And whereas only the great nobles of Corenwald had been invited to Darrow's treaty feast, the feechie feast was for the whole band, right down to the littlest wee-feechies.

There were no entertainers at the banquet. The feechies entertained themselves with games and frolics of various sorts—tree-climbing contests, fire-jumping contests, a spitting contest (which Mrs. Turtlebane won), vine-swinging exhibitions, and the most ferocious wrestling matches Aidan had ever seen. Also, a few good-natured fistfights broke out, which was the custom at all feechie celebrations.

Just as the games and contests seemed to be winding down, Aidan heard whooping and yodeling out in the swamp. Then the feechie feasters began a rhythmic chant:

Alligator, grabble-gator
Welcome to the feast.
Catch a gator, snatch a gator,
Scaly, scary beast.
Rassle gator, hassle gator
Boss of all the swamp.
Tug a gator, hug a gator,
Stomp and romp and chomp.
Tussle gator, russle gator,
Welcome to the feast.
Grip a gator, flip a gator,
Scaly, scary beast.

The feechies had whipped themselves into a frenzy with their chanting when an eleven-foot alligator charged into the crowd, pursued by five or six feechie boys waving pine-knot torches. The alligator feared nothing besides fire, and now that he had the campfire in front of him and the torch fires behind him, he had nowhere left to run. He hissed and growled, lunged and snapped at the feechies who encircled him.

The "gator grabble" was the highlight of the evening's entertainment. It was a simple enough game. Odo Watersnake had made a "grabbling vine"—a loop woven from forest vines. Using a branch that was long enough to keep him out of the alligator's reach, Odo looped the grabbling vine over the alligator's head so that he wore it like a necklace. The object of the game was simply to remove the grabbling vine from the alligator's head, using one's bare hands.

Everyone seemed to have his or her own technique for getting at the grabbling vine. Most involved sneaking up behind the alligator. But an alligator's bulging eyes see behind as well as they see in front, and every time someone came at him from behind, the alligator whipped around and sent the contestant scrambling long before he got close enough to snatch the vine. Some contestants worked in pairs, one distracting the alligator, the other reaching in for the grabbling vine. But even in that case, the alligator had little trouble putting both feechies to flight. Benno Frogger, always something of a show-off, had a technique that involved coming at the alligator from the side in a diving somersault. But this method was more glamorous than effective; he was no more successful than the rest.

Most of the feechiefolk had taken a turn—all the he-feechies, most of the she-feechies, and even a few wee-feechies. It appeared that the alligator might go back into the swamp still wearing the grabbling vine. But then it was Aidan's turn.

Aidan leaped onto the alligator's back, just as he had leaped onto Samson's back, in that safe place right behind the alligator's head, where neither snapping jaws nor thrashing tail could reach him. From that perch, he took his time untying the vine from around the alligator's neck, in spite of the alligator's thrashing gyrations. When Aidan handed the grabbling vine to Chief Gergo, the crowd whooped and cheered. More than once he heard himself described in the most glowing terms the feechies knew: "That young civilizer's got what it takes!"

By this time, the food was ready. The fare was not as sumptuous as the food served at Darrow's treaty feast, but Aidan was famished after such a day as this, and he ate heartily and gratefully. Rather than plates, the feechies used mats of tightly woven palmetto fronds. The meal began with a salad of wild purple lettuces and leaves from the sweet bay tree. There were plums and mayhaws and citron melons. The catfish caught by the fishing parties had been cooked in the fire and brought out on bamboo sticks. The highlight of the meal—for the feechies, at least—was the serving of the lizard eggs. They had been buried for six months and dug up for the occasion, now that they were good and rotten. The feechies considered this a delicacy. Aidan considered the rotten eggs disgusting.

As the feasters were finishing their dessert of roasted acorns, Gergo rose to his feet. "Friends," he began, "we're here to jubilate a new friend."

All eyes turned to Aidan. Gergo continued his speech. "Aidan of the Tam been doing things today that we didn't think a civilizer could do. He heard the feechie watch-out bark and didn't run off. He caught the biggest catfish ever cooked and ate at a feechie feast—and not the civilizer way either, all finicky with a pole and hook, but with his bare hands. He won the gator grabble. There ain't no question: This civilizer has got what it takes." The crowd cheered and hollered and stomped on the soft ground of the Meeting Hummock. When the feechies settled down again, Gergo continued.

"But Aidan of the Tam is our guest tonight because he did something else we never thought we'd see a civilizer do: He saved a feechie's life. He wasn't paying no attention to his own safety when he rescued our Dobro Turtlebane from a panther." More cheering erupted all around the Meeting Hummock.

"And that's why I declare that Aidan of the Tam is a feechiefriend, with all the rights and privileges that are due to a feechiefriend—that is to say, his fights is our fights, and our fights is his'n." The crowd cheered again. "Hooray for the civilizer," and "Three cheers for Aidan of the Tam!"

"A feechiefriend has to have a feechie name," continued the old chief. "Aidan killed a panther. His feechie name will be Pantherbane—Aidan Pantherbane."

Gergo motioned for Dobro to come to the forefront. He removed the panther cape from Dobro's shoulders and, placing it on Aidan's shoulders, he said, "It's time we gave this panther cape to the person it belongs to."

The chieftain then nodded to Rabbo and Jonko, who brought stone pots containing a soupy mixture of gray swamp mud. They slathered the mud all over Aidan. It gave him the exact complexion of the feechiefolk. "This keeps the bugs off," explained Gergo. Aidan wished he had had it earlier in the day, when the yellow flies were attacking. "It gives you a better color too," Gergo added.

"And now," said Chief Gergo, "there's one last thing." He motioned Aidan over to a stump that had been covered with a mat of palmetto fronds like a table-cloth. "Kneel down here and place your arm across this stump, with your palm facing up. Relax as much as you can. This is going to burn a little bit."

Gergo nodded at Odo Watersnake, who was standing beside the fire. Odo reached a pair of bone tongs into a pile of orange coals at the fire's edge. He pulled out a smoking chunk of carved limestone. Aidan watched nervously as Odo approached him, and he had to muster willpower he didn't even know he had to keep from pulling his arm away as Odo pressed the burning stone against the underside of his forearm. Aidan bit his lip to keep from screaming as it seared his skin. He couldn't keep the tears from streaming down his face.

When Odo pulled the stone away, Gergo quickly poured a slimy substance over Aidan's forearm and massaged it into the burn. To Aidan's astonishment, the pain in his arm melted away. He inspected his forearm. Though he couldn't feel the burn anymore, it had left a mark: an angry red scar, about as long as Aidan's finger, in the precise shape of an alligator with open jaws and a curling tail.

"Now you bear the feechiemark," announced Gergo. "You'll bear it all your life. Any feechie who sees this mark will know that you are a feechiefriend, and they'll be a friend to you."

Gergo extended a hand to Aidan and helped him to his feet. He straightened the panther cape on Aidan's shoulders, turned him to face the feechiefolk, and raised Aidan's arm to show the feechiemark on his forearm. "Aidan Pantherbane," he shouted. "Feechiefriend."

The feechiefolk answered with one voice: "Aidan Pantherbane, feechiefriend. His fights is our fights, and our fights is his'n!"

The feechie feast continued well into the night, though the guest of honor missed much of it. Exhausted from his travels and the day's trials, Aidan excused himself from the revels soon after the feechiefriend ceremony. Benno Frogger showed him to a vine hammock high in the crown of a live oak. There Aidan slept, just as soundly as if he were home in his own bed, blissfully unaware of the raucous whooping, arguing, singing, laughing, caterwauling, and general merrymaking below.

Chapter Seventeen

Battle Camp

The next morning, Aidan was up with the sun, anxious to continue his journey upstream to the lime sink and on to the Bonifay Plain. Very few of the feechies were awake to see him off, and those few were awake only because they hadn't yet gone to bed.

Dobro had dozed his way through the night, leaning against the base of the oak tree where Aidan slept. He insisted on guiding Aidan on his journey as far as the Western Road. Aidan was only too glad to let him, both because he would enjoy the company and because he couldn't possibly find his way otherwise.

For most of the trip, they traveled the feechie way—swinging vine to vine, leaping branch to branch through the treetops. With his mud-gray skin and flying panther cape, Aidan looked like a native feechie. Aidan performed treetop acrobatics he would have never attempted alone. But he watched Dobro intently, putting his hands precisely where Dobro put his hands, leaping to the precise spots where Dobro leaped, and they progressed through the forest at a clip that Aidan wouldn't have believed possible. There was still an hour left before noon when the boys stopped to rest in a tree overhanging the limestone sink that gave rise to Bayberry Creek.

The Western Road was in sight. Here on the verge of the civilizers' world the two friends would have to go their separate ways.

Dobro stared absently at the green water fifteen feet below. He spoke for the first time since they had left the Meeting Hummock. "I don't see why you couldn't stay with us a little bit longer. We was having a good time, wasn't we?"

"Sure we were," Aidan answered. "I had the time of my life. But the battle for Corenwald is on. I can't be off frolicking in the swamp with the feechiefolk while my brothers are fighting—maybe even dying—on the battlefield."

"Then how 'bout I go with you?" said Dobro excitedly. "Your fights is my fights now."

"Not this fight. This is between the Corenwalders and the Pyrthens."

Dobro looked hurt. "You don't think I'm a Corenwalder? You don't think them was Corenwalders you spent yesterday evening with?"

Aidan paused to think. "No, Dobro, I don't suppose I ever thought of the feechiefolk as Corenwalders."

"The feechiefolk was Corenwalders many long years before you civilizers come to this island." Dobro lifted his head and looked westward toward the battle plain. "You might be right. This battle you're headed to might be none of my business. It might just be one bunch of civilizers fighting another bunch of civilizers to decide who gets to pretend this island belongs to them. That's a fight you can keep for your own."

Dobro turned and looked Aidan in the eye. "But if

your fight is a fight for Corenwald, that's a whole other thing. You love Corenwald. I know you do. But you don't love it no more than we do."

A short silence prevailed between the boys. Dobro had given Aidan a whole new way of looking at things. "There's an old prophecy in the feechie lore," Dobro continued. "It tells about a civilizer king who's going to make one nation out of Corenwald. There won't be no civilizer Corenwald or no feechie Corenwald . . . just Corenwald.

"Most of the feechiefolk don't pay no mind to that old story. They think it's make-believe—just something to tell the wee-feechies. Most of the feechiefolks wouldn't even want to join up with the civilizers. But I been keeping an eye out for that civilizer king. When he shows up, I'm going to be the first feechie to join up with him."

Dobro gave Aidan a sidelong glance, as if he weren't saying everything he was thinking. "But it's probably time you got going," he said, and he shoved Aidan off the tree limb and into the water below. When Aidan came up for air, he heard Dobro deep in the forest: *Ha-ha-ha-hrawffff-wooooooooo . . . Ha-ha-ha-hrawffff-wooooooooo.*

Aidan's coating of mud was dissolving into a gray cloud in the green water of the limestone sink. He rubbed away the last of the mud on his face and arms as he swam lazily to the edge of the sink. Climbing onto the grass, he found his flour sack, safe and dry. Dobro, nimble as a pickpocket, had snatched the sack away from Aidan as he fell and dropped it on the grassy bank. Aidan took off his panther cape, shook it dry as best he could, then folded it and placed it in the flour sack. Now that he was out of the creek bottom forest, it was time to become a civilizer again. He shouldered the flour sack and headed down the Western Road, energized by the thought of seeing his brothers among the mighty men of Corenwald.

‡ ‡ ‡

Aidan had never seen a real battle camp before. But in daydreams during those long afternoons in the sheep pastures, he had fought many battles and spent many nights encamped with the armies of Corenwald. His head was filled with clashing arms, with battles and sieges and cavalry charges. Though he was a shepherd boy, Aidan's heart was the heart of a warrior. So when he crested a gentle rise and caught his first glimpse of the Corenwalders' battle camp a league westward on the Bonifay Plain, a thrill surged through his every bone and sinew. At the same time, though, he felt an odd familiarity, as if he were back home after a long time away.

Even from this distance, Aidan could see that the encampment looked just the way he had thought it would. Blue-and-gold battle flags rippled lazily in the slight breeze. A thousand field tents pitched in long ranks, the distant whinny of a warhorse, even the smoke drifting up from the remains of the noonday cooking fires—all of these things he had imagined and longed for. The early afternoon sun glinted off the helmets and spear points of a dozen pairs of sentries standing guard around the camp's perimeter. They looked so strong and splendid that it made Aidan's heart hurt with pride to think that he was their countryman.

A small valley ran along the camp's western edge—the opposite edge from where Aidan stood. A bank of chalky clay led down ten or fifteen feet to a grassy flat where a river had run many years before. On the other side of the valley stood the Pyrthen camp, its black-and-red battle flags raised high. Beyond it, as far as the bottomland forest along the Eechihoolee River, stretched the plain, treeless except for the occasional cedar planted by farmers who had farmed here decades earlier.

It was hard to tell from such a distance, but the Pyrthen camp seemed to be much larger than the Corenwalder camp. If the Corenwalders had a thousand tents, the Pyrthens, it appeared, had two thousand, perhaps even three thousand. Not good odds. *Well, then,* thought Aidan, *all the more glorious shall the Corenwalder victory be!* He tossed the bag over his shoulder and broke into a quick trot for the last league of his journey.

‡ ‡ ‡

At the edge of the Corenwalder camp, two sentries stood on either side of the path. They were dressed in the plate mail and blue tunics of Corenwalder foot soldiers. One of the sentries was tall and thin, with a wispy mustache and a bashful little chin that didn't protrude quite as far as the Adam's apple just below it. The other was a round little fellow who barely came up to the top of his partner's breastplate. The Corenwalder army hadn't made any uniforms for men his size and shape—or, in any case, he didn't get one. Aidan had to admit that these soldiers looked much more impressive from a league away than they did up close.

The sentries were leaning on their spears and appeared to be deep in conversation. They hadn't noticed that Aidan had walked up on them. He cleared his throat loudly to get their attention. They stood up straight and pointed their spears in his direction.

In unison they spoke. "Halt! Who goes there?"

Aidan smiled at the sentries and spoke in a confident, soldierly tone, as to his equals. "I am Aidan Errolson of Longleaf Manor, loyal subject to King Darrow and brother to four warriors of Corenwald."

The sentries turned their heads toward each other, then burst into laughter. The tall one spoke first. "Warriors of Corenwald? Well, they ain't been doing no warrioring around here, I can tell you that!"

Aidan was perplexed. He looked about him. "Isn't this the battle camp of the Corenwalders? Aren't those Corenwald's battle flags flying overhead?"

The short sentry looked skyward, shielding his eyes from the afternoon sun. "Hey, Terence, young Aidan Errolson has a point. Those *are* battle flags."

"Well, I'll be," answered Terence. "I thought King Darrow was drying his laundry." He snorted with laughter, almost before he had finished the joke. His short, round partner laughed a wheezing laugh and slapped his knee.

Aidan couldn't believe what he was hearing. These soldiers were mocking the very king they were sworn to serve—the king who had provided them with arms and armor. He thought it best to go on his way and leave them to their hilarity. "May I pass?"

"Not so fast." It was Terence, the tall jokester again. "Lester, this being a battle camp and all, don't you think we should interrogate the subject?"

"Right, right," said Lester. He assumed an official-looking posture. "State your name."

"It's Aidan Errolson. I already told you."

"Yes. Of course. Aidan Errolson of the Fighting Errolsons. Brother to four warriors." Terence stifled a giggle.

Lester resumed the interrogation. "State your business."

"I'm here to see my brothers—to deliver this sack of provisions from home and to get news of their well-being to bring home to our father."

Terence snorted at this. "News of their well-being! You can tell Daddy that unless one of the Fighting Errolsons burned himself at his cooking fire or broke a fingernail while polishing up his armor, he's as safe in this battle camp as a babe in arms."

Lester broke in. "And as for that sack of provisions, we'd be glad to deliver it to your brothers, so you just hand it over and run along home." He reached for the sack. But by this time, Aidan had had enough of these soldiers and their jokes. He drew back the hand that was holding the sack and glared at the sentries. Though the soldiers were bigger, older, and certainly better armed, they could see that the young shepherd boy meant business. They decided not to press the issue.

"*Ahem.* Well, I reckon we could let you deliver the sack—this time—but you better let us have a look inside."

"Yeah, we can't be allowing parcels to enter the encampment without performing a visual inspection." Terence had learned this official-sounding language during his brief training.

This seemed a reasonable request. Aidan untied the drawstring at the mouth of the sack and folded back the coarse cloth so the sentries could see inside. "It's loaves of bread and new cheeses from our goats."

"Look, Terence—cheese! Young Aidan of the Fighting Errolsons is bringing cheese to his warrior brothers!"

"You know what they say," answered Terence. "Nothing fortifies a man's warrior spirit like a nice fresh goat cheese." This was just too much for Terence. He doubled over laughing at his own joke. Lester, too, was nearly incapacitated with laughter. They leaned on each other, whinnying and guffawing.

Aidan was puzzled by the men's behavior. Their hilarity was all out of proportion to the joke, which just wasn't that funny. He had seen people laugh extra hard at little jokes during times of particular jollity—at the solstice festival, for instance, or at the harvest feast, when a summer's long, hot labor was finally at an end. But Aidan could see that these men were not laughing from an excess of joy. Theirs was a forced laughter, with too much breath and not enough belly. They laughed the way a person laughs when he has slipped and fallen in front of strangers and wants to show he's not embarrassed, even though he is.

Aidan cinched up his sack, slung it back over his shoulder, and continued into the camp. If the sentries wished to stop him, they were free to do so. But he had no intention of waiting for them to regain their composure, and they had no intention of stopping him.

As he entered the encampment, Aidan realized the sentries had been right about one thing at least: Though there were uniformed soldiers milling about and battle flags flapping overhead, this did not feel like a battle camp. There was no buzz of excitement as he had expected. He did not hear the hum and clank of last-minute battle preparations—no blacksmiths pounding at swords and spears, no mighty men strapping on their armor, no pageboys gearing up the warhorses. There were no soldiers nursing wounds from battles already fought. He saw no units drilling in the common areas. And in the faces of the soldiers he saw neither grim determination nor the swelling pride of conquest, nor even the fear of death. Instead, he saw heavy-lidded indifference. They looked more like men about to go to sleep than men about to go to war.

Aidan saw a few signs of life and vigor among the Corenwalders, but they weren't very encouraging. A particularly animated supply officer beat a pack mule that had stopped in the passage. The next tent row over, an officer and a foot soldier yelled and swore at each other. Behind one of the tents, a knot of soldiers huddled together, talking excitedly and pointing intently at a spot on the ground between them. Aidan thought they must have a map, going over a battle scheme or planning a raid on the enemy camp. But as he drew near, he realized they were throwing dice, gambling away their soldiers' wages.

Aidan wandered down one tent row, then another, searching for his brothers but without success. Few of the men he passed acknowledged his presence at all. No one noticed that he was lost and confused, nor did anyone help him find his way.

Aidan was feeling very discouraged when he heard a voice beside him.

"You look lost."

Aidan turned to see a boy about his age wearing the hat and side pouch of a messenger. The messenger boy had fallen into step with Aidan and was holding out his hand to shake. "I'm Herschel," he said, showing Aidan the first genuine smile he had seen since arriving at the camp.

Aidan shook Herschel's hand. "I'm Aidan."

"What are you looking for?" asked the messenger boy.

"My brothers. The Errolsons."

"Everything around here is arranged by shires," said Herschel. "What shire are you from?"

"Hustingshire."

"Oh, you're almost there," Herschel answered. He pointed over to his right. "The Hustingshire regiment is two tent rows over."

"Thanks," said Aidan, shaking the messenger boy's hand. He started to leave in the direction Herschel had pointed, but he stopped. "Herschel?" he asked. "Can I ask you one thing?"

"Sure."

"What is going on here?"

"How do you mean?"

"Look around you. Look at the soldiers in this battle camp. They don't look like the mighty men of Corenwald. These aren't the faces of the free and the true. What's bothering everybody?"

Herschel chuckled and shook his head. "You mean you haven't heard what's bothering everybody?"

"How could I have heard?" Aidan answered him. "Except for a couple of smart-aleck guards, you're the first person who's said a word to me since I set foot in this camp."

Herschel looked up at the sun. He appeared to be judging the time of day from its position in the sky. "You'll find out soon," he said. "Within the hour, you'll see for yourself what's bothering everybody."

Chapter Eighteen
A Challenge

Herschel the messenger boy went about his business, and Aidan found his brothers right where Herschel said he would. They were seated on logs around the cooking pit in front of their tent. Aidan was overjoyed to see them.

"Brennus! Maynard!" he shouted eagerly. "Jasper! Percy!" His brothers just stared at him.

"You should see your faces!" he continued. "Are you that surprised to see me? You should have known I'd figure out some way to get here." He began opening his bag. "I wouldn't let you have all the fun yourselves. Now, who wants some of Ebbe's new cheese and Moira's fresh bread?"

Aidan was so busy talking and unwrapping that he didn't notice Brennus's and Maynard's surprised looks narrow into scowls. Even Jasper and Percy were frowning.

Aidan went on, oblivious. "You have to tell me everything that has happened since you've been here. Father's doing better, I'm glad to say, but it was getting pretty—"

"What are you doing here?" sneered Brennus, cutting Aidan off in midsentence. "Don't you have some sheep to tend to?"

"Or some feechies to fight?" added Maynard.

"Funny you should mention that," answered Aidan. "You wouldn't believe the day I had yesterday—"

"You shouldn't be here!" shouted Brennus, interrupting him again. "You just came to watch us all get killed. Why did Father let you come?"

"What did I do?" asked Aidan. There was hurt in his voice. "What did I say?" None of his brothers would answer him or even look at him. Aidan looked from one brother's face to the next, searching for any clue that would tell him what was going on.

Then a trumpet blast split the air, followed by wild shouts. The sounds came from the west, the direction of the Pyrthen camp. Was it a raid? Was the battle beginning? Aidan looked to his brothers, expecting them to arm themselves and rush out to join the fray. But they didn't. Brennus uttered a long sigh and cast his eyes heavenward. Percy held his head in his hands; he was covering his ears. Maynard and Jasper sat stone-faced, as if they had heard nothing.

Surprised that his brothers seemed to have no intention of going anywhere, Aidan leaped to his feet. He motioned for his brothers to come along and ran in the direction of the shouts. He was already well on his way when he heard Percy's voice behind him. "Aidan! Don't go there. It's not safe!"

Aidan ran to the edge of the valley that bordered the battle camp. On the opposite edge, in front of a great oak tree, stood a line of thirty or forty men in black armor and black, spiked helmets—Pyrthen foot soldiers bearing spears and blood-red shields.

In the middle of the line stood the biggest man Aidan had ever seen. He looked to be seven feet tall, maybe taller, and a huge plume on top of his helmet added another two feet to his height. The tallest of the other men barely came up to his chin. He looked like an oversized iron statue of a man. His right hand clutched a twelve-foot spear. His left arm was strapped into a shield like a full moon, four feet in diameter, and decorated with images of the Pyrthen gods in all their cruelty and hideousness. Over his left shoulder was the double blade of a massive battle-ax, its handle stuck into a sheath strapped to his back. Even from across the valley, Aidan could see the cruel, murderous look in the great warrior's eyes.

The Pyrthen's deep voice thundered across the valley. "Dogs of Corenwald! I am Greidawl of Pyrth. Send a champion to face me in single combat, in full view of our two armies. If he triumphs over me, the army of Pyrth will be defeated, and we will be your slaves. If I triumph, the Corenwalders will be defeated, and you will be slaves to us."

The Pyrthen champion paused, pretending to be waiting for an answer from the sentries on the valley's eastern edge. Receiving none, he spoke again. "You have nothing to lose. You are our slaves already. Every day you tremble at my threats, every day you swallow my taunts without response, you show that you are slaves to Pyrth and servants to our gods.

"Through two phases of the moon, I have stood each day on this hill and made you this offer. Why should your whole army be put to the sword when the blood of one man would do? Is there not a single man among you, dogs of Corenwald?

"I am Greidawl of Pyrth. Here I stand, by the power of the Pyrthen gods. By their power I have broken men like twigs. By their power I have mown men down like autumn wheat. By whose power do you slink and cower? Can the God of Corenwald raise up a champion to face me? Who would spare the blood of his brothers?"

Greidawl finished his speech and stood with arms outstretched in a gesture of mock welcome. Behind him, the Pyrthen soldiers waved and jeered and climbed around in the lower limbs of the oak tree like deranged monkeys. On the other side of the valley, the Corenwalders looked at their fingernails and drew in the dirt with their toes. They were too ashamed to look at each other, and they dared not look in the direction of the gigantic Pyrthen. Finally, they began to trickle back to their tents.

Greidawl threw back his head and laughed a loud, throaty laugh. The plume on the top of his helmet danced a derisive jig. The mere sight of him terrorized Aidan, even from across the valley. Now he saw why the Corenwalders were so demoralized. This was what had robbed them of their manly courage.

Aidan walked back to his brothers' tent. The seats where he had left them were now unoccupied, so Aidan opened the tent flap and peered in. There they sat, in the hot, stuffy dimness. No one was speaking. All eyes were fixed on the ground in sullen stares.

Percy was the first to speak. "For two weeks now, he has come each afternoon to the valley's edge and made the same offer. If we send a champion out to fight him man to man, we can avoid a battle between the armies. If Greidawl wins, we become the slaves of Corenwald. If the Corenwalder wins, the Pyrthen fighters become our slaves."

"So who's going forth, and when?" asked Aidan. "Let's see . . . maybe Wilson Longshanks? He's not as big as Greidawl, but he's the biggest soldier we've got. Or Leonard Stout? He can pick up a young bull. How about Wendell Quick? He's not big, but I'm sure he could dance circles around that lumbering oaf."

Brennus interrupted: "Listen, Aidan Dull-witted. Nobody's going out to face that monster."

"What do you mean? He stood right there and insulted our entire army, our king, and our God."

"What is anybody going to do about it?" Brennus answered. "Didn't you notice? He's seven feet tall. His legs are like tree trunks. No, his *arms* are like tree trunks. His legs are like . . . they're like . . ." He struggled for a comparison.

"Like bigger tree trunks?" offered Percy.

Brennus glared at him. "His legs are like pillars. His broadsword is as long as my spear. His spear is as long and as thick as a pine sapling. It would pierce a shield as if it were a sycamore leaf. But in his hand, it's like a reed."

"But surely he can't move very quickly," offered Aidan.

"He doesn't have to. His armor is iron; a normal man could hardly pick it up, yet he wears it as easily as I wear my tunic. He could take blow after blow and never feel a thing—though no soldier has ever lived to strike him twice. They say he's killed a thousand men. He's invincible."

"No," said Aidan. "Only the One God is invincible."

"Then perhaps the One God should meet him in the field," Brennus shot back.

Brennus's irreverent remark hung in the air. No one quite knew how to answer the eldest brother. He seemed a little ashamed of himself.

Aidan broke the silence. "Let's assume, then, that we can't find a warrior to face the Pyrthen champion man to man. What would happen if we mounted an offensive and fought the Pyrthens army to army?"

"We'd get slaughtered," answered Brennus. "That's what would happen. They have us outnumbered two to one. They have superior arms and armor. And they're hardened veterans. We're mostly farmers. We can't possibly defeat them."

"So we just sit here and wait until the Pyrthens are ready to destroy us?" Aidan challenged. "And in the meantime, we just receive insults and blasphemy from this monster every single day, without giving him answer? Do King Darrow and his generals have no better plan than this?"

"Not so far as we know," answered Maynard, gloomily. "But at least we're not all dead."

"But isn't this a kind of death?" Aidan's terror at the sight of Greidawl had given way to indignation. He was ashamed at the cowardice of his brothers and countrymen. "You die every day you hear that beast insult our armies, mock our king, and blaspheme the One God. You die every day you submit to a slavery that has been imposed on you without a fight."

Brennus, sullen before, was growing red in the face. "The Pyrthens haven't enslaved us!"

"You're right," replied Aidan. "We have enslaved ourselves. We weren't born slaves. We were born to serve only God and king. But look outside this tent. Look at Corenwald's fighting men. Those aren't the faces of free men. They can't even meet the eyes of a stranger. Defeat and humiliation stare out from every face. And not one blow has been struck! We live under the protection of the One True God. Our enemies worship statues of fish and snakes! And yet we bow to their yoke without a fight?

"You don't want to be killed. I don't either. But wouldn't you rather die once than die every day of your life?"

Brennus leaned across, his face just inches from Aidan's. "Then perhaps you should go have your one good death tomorrow afternoon when the giant comes back."

"Maybe I will," said Aidan. Shouldering his flour sack, he stood up to leave.

"Aidan, wait!" It was Percy. "Don't be stupid. You can't fight Greidawl."

"Let him go," said Brennus. "He can't help being stupid. And as for his fighting the giant, there's little danger of that. I doubt our brother the shepherd boy is braver than the entire Corenwalder army."

Brennus glared at his youngest brother. Aidan shook his head, then lifted the tent flap. Without another word, he stepped into the slanting sunlight, not sure what to do next.

Chapter Nineteen

A Champion Appears

It was late afternoon when Aidan left his brothers' tent. He decided he might as well just go back home to Longleaf. There seemed nothing else for him to do in the battle camp; he had delivered the parcels to his brothers, and he could report back to Father that they were in good health. But this wasn't at all what he had imagined.

Though there were still two hours of daylight left, Aidan decided it was best to find an out-of-the-way place where he could lie down and sleep out the night before heading home in the morning. It had been an exhausting couple of days. He wandered through the camp, hardly even looking at the soldiers who stood in idle groups outside their tents. These men had been his heroes, the mighty men of Corenwald; now he could hardly bear the sight of them.

It was going to be a warm, cloudless night; Aidan would need no tent over his head. He picked a spot between two tents, underneath the tent ropes. He spread out the flour sack beneath him and used his panther cape for a cover. A chunk of firewood served as his pillow. By the time the evening star first appeared, he was sound asleep.

But Aidan's sleep grew fitful around midnight, when the camp was perfectly still and he was assailed by dreams. He dreamed of a Corenwald ruled by the Pyrthen Empire. He dreamed of the black-and-red banners of Pyrth fluttering over Tambluff Castle. He dreamed of live oaks felled and hewn into ribs for Pyrthen warships, of the singing longleaf pines planed to beams for Emperor Mareddud's newest palace. He dreamed of swamps drained, of feechiefolk in chains. He dreamed of the manor house burning once again.

Aidan's homeland was a dark and unhappy place in those dreams. But then, just before daybreak, he had a dream of a different sort: a dream of salvation. He dreamed of the Wilderking, coming out of the swamps to deliver Corenwald from her enemies. He wore a panther-hide cape.

Aidan woke with a start as the sun first peeped over the eastern horizon. He had a long way to go and was anxious to begin his journey home. But even though he was wide awake, his dreams of the previous night still troubled him. What did they mean? Did they mean anything at all?

Except for the sentries and others with predawn duties, few soldiers were up and moving as Aidan made his way through the encampment back toward the Western Road. But Aidan recognized a familiar face as he passed by one of the few fires lit at that hour. Herschel, the messenger boy from the day before, sat hugging his knees and staring bleary-eyed into the fire.

"Herschel," called Aidan, "it's me, Aidan Errolson. You helped me find my brothers yesterday."

It took Herschel a second to free his attention from the fire's hypnotic pull. "Aidan," he answered, and motioned toward the fire. "Come, warm up."

Aidan squatted beside the messenger boy and held his palms out toward the fire. "You don't look like you slept very well," he remarked.

"True enough," answered Herschel. "I spent most of the night planning my future: a long life of slavery or a violent death sometime in the immediate future. That didn't leave much time for sleeping."

"Don't talk like that," said Aidan. "Yesterday, you were the only person I could find in this whole camp who hadn't let that big-mouthed Pyrthen get to you. Now you're acting like everybody else."

"I know things today that I didn't know yesterday."

"What sort of things?" asked Aidan.

Herschel looked around, then leaned in close to whisper. "Yesterday afternoon, just after Greidawl finished his daily performance, I delivered a message to the Pyrthen camp."

"And . . . ?"

"And King Darrow is trying to surrender."

The words hit Aidan like a fist to the stomach. His ears rang; bright spots appeared in front of his face. Would Corenwald end like this? Would his countrymen not even go down fighting?

Aidan managed to catch his breath. "What do you mean King Darrow is *trying* to surrender?" he asked. "Either you surrender or you don't."

"The Pyrthen commander said he would accept surrender only from a defeated foe."

Aidan blinked. He didn't follow Herschel's meaning.

"It means there is going to be a battle," explained Herschel. "Either a single combat between two champions or a pitched battle between the armies. We have three days to find a champion to fight Greidawl. If no Corenwalder champion appears, the Pyrthen army attacks on the third day."

Both boys were silent as Aidan digested this information. Aidan remembered his dreams of the previous night—of Corenwald subjugated and Corenwald delivered. He remembered Bayard's advice: *Live the life that unfolds before you. Love goodness more than you fear evil.*

At last Aidan spoke. "Herschel, I have a plan."

"Does it involve running away and not stopping until you're far, far from this place? That's the plan I've been working on."

Aidan ignored him. "I need a pen and some paper to write on."

"You're writing your will? Probably a good idea. Look in my pouch."

Aidan found pen, ink, and palmetto paper in Herschel's messenger pouch. He quickly wrote a note and, folding it in two, nodded toward Herschel. "Can you take me to King Darrow?"

"King Darrow?" exclaimed Herschel. "Are you crazy? Don't you suppose the king's got a lot on his mind?"

"Just point me in the right direction."

Herschel watched Aidan carefully for a few seconds, just to be sure he was serious. Herschel rose to his feet and, brushing firewood bark from his tunic, stepped out into the alley between the tent rows. "Come on, then," he said, waving his hand for Aidan to follow.

"The king is always in the council tent," said Herschel as the two boys walked through the awakening camp. "All day, every day, he's in there with his generals and closest advisers. Some nights, he even sleeps there."

Near the camp's center, Herschel pointed to a circle of large tents. Within the circle of tents were four or five larger tents. "That's the command yard," he said. "If you get past those two guards, the council tent is the biggest one inside the command yard. I don't know what you're up to. I don't even want to know. So I'm going to head back to my tent and let you do what you think you need to do." With that, he turned and walked back the way he came, slowly shaking his head and looking once or twice over his shoulder.

Aidan took a deep breath as he prepared to face the guards at the entrance to the command yard. They were tall, strong men, square of jaw and stout of limb. Unlike the guards Aidan had encountered the previous day at the edge of camp, these were professional soldiers, the king's own bodyguard. As Aidan approached, their straight-ahead stare never changed. They maintained the same impassive expression as the boy spoke. "Ahem, pardon me, I have a note for King Darrow."

Neither of the guards acknowledged him. Aidan spoke a little louder. "I have a note for King Darrow." No response. "A champion has presented himself . . . to face the Pyrthen champion." At this, the guards looked at one another. One of them nodded, and the other reached out a hand toward Aidan. Aidan gave the paper to the guard, who disappeared into the tent. Neither of the guards had spoken a word.

"I'll just wait here," called Aidan to the tent flap.

Three or four minutes later, the guard emerged from the tent. "The king will see you," he said. Aidan followed the guard into the tent, then into another tent inside the first, the inner chamber of the council tent. Here, surrounded by charts and maps and battlefield models sat King Darrow in a chair, along with seven or eight generals and noblemen.

Aidan looked at the men around the table. He had seen most of them at Longleaf at one time or another. His own father, no doubt, would have been among this group if not for his stroke. Then Aidan's mouth dropped open in astonishment. At King Darrow's right hand sat a barrel-chested old man with blazing white hair and green eyes that seemed to see more deeply than any others'. On the ground in front of him sat two goats, a billy and a nanny. He had cut his hair and cleaned himself up, but there was no question: this was Bayard the Truthspeaker sitting at the right hand of the king himself, in the seat of the chief adviser.

Aidan stared at the prophet in disbelief. Bayard's expression, on the other hand, did not betray the least bit of surprise. Rather, the little smile, the raised eyebrows, the upward tilt of the head all said, as clearly as if he had spoken: "Ah, there you are, young Aidan Errolson. I knew you'd come soon."

The voice of the king brought Aidan back to reality. Darrow held Aidan's note in front of him and was reading out loud:

Your Majesty—

I will fight the Pyrthen champion and so spare the shedding of any additional Corenwalder blood. You determine the time and place, and I will be there to fight for Corenwald.

Yours sincerely,
Aidan Errolson of Longleaf Manor

The king looked over the paper at Aidan. "And our champion, this Aidan Errolson, why has he sent a messenger boy instead of coming himself?"

"Well, Your Majesty, you see, I—" began Aidan.

"Errol's eldest son is named Brennus, is he not?" interrupted the king.

"Yes, Sire," answered Aidan, "Brennus is the eldest of the brothers."

"So this Aidan is the second Errolson?"

"The fifth, Your Majesty," answered Aidan.

"The fifth? No, no, you must be confused. Errol's fifth son would be no bigger than you are."

"True enough, Sire. I *am* Aidan Errolson."

The king looked again at the signature on the letter and gave a short bark of surprise. "You can't be serious!"

Bayard smiled and spoke to the king. "Oh, he's serious, Your Majesty. I've met Aidan Errolson; this is he."

Darrow turned toward the prophet at his right hand. "But he can't face the Pyrthens' champion." He turned back to Aidan. "Boy, have you seen this Greidawl?"

"I have seen him, Your Majesty. I have heard of his cruelty and the thousand men he has slain. But I also know him to be a boaster and a blasphemer against the One True God."

King Darrow shook his head. "I admire your bravery, lad, but you cannot possibly—" The king broke off; the whole idea was so ridiculous he didn't even finish his sentence.

Aidan stood a little straighter. His face was set in a steely gaze of determination. "Your Majesty, I cannot hear our enemies speak against Corenwald and the One God without giving answer."

There was an unspoken rebuke in Aidan's response—a rebuke against the king who had yet to answer Greidawl and whose cowardice had brought his kingdom to the brink of ruin. Darrow heard this rebuke, and it angered him. "Insolent boy!" he said through clenched teeth. He pointed toward the tent entrance. "Go home where you belong! There you won't have to hear the giant's taunts."

Aidan stood his ground. "If I go home, Your Majesty, I should hear Greidawl's taunts all the more. I should become like the soldiers outside this tent, who hear the Pyrthen's voice so clearly that they cannot hear the voice of God."

Darrow looked away. "Away with you, boy. Go home. I have much to think about." His voice was softer now. "I don't need the blood of children on my hands."

Aidan looked to Bayard for help. But Bayard was silent. He just sat with that faint smile on his face. When two guards approached Aidan from either side to escort him out, Aidan grew desperate. "Your Majesty," he blurted out, "I know you've tried to surrender to the Pyrthens!" The guards stopped in their tracks and looked to Darrow, not sure what to do. Aidan continued, "And I know the Pyrthens insist on a battle."

The king sat stone-faced, neither confirming nor denying Aidan's claims.

"Sire," continued Aidan, "if you have already given up hope of defeating the Pyrthens, either army to army or champion to champion, what would it hurt if I faced Greidawl? Do you have a soldier who can defeat him?"

Darrow was silent still. One of his generals spoke up at last. "Your Majesty, the boy has a point. We cannot defeat the Pyrthens in a pitched battle. We have no fighting man who could hope to defeat the Pyrthens' champion in single combat. The boy's offer may be the best we can hope for. The Pyrthens will have the blood they require, and we will lose no soldiers."

"If the boy wishes to die for Corenwald," added Lord Selwyn, "why not let him?"

Darrow looked into the face of each member of his War Council, one after the other. In his turn, each man nodded, a barely perceptible nod with eyes averted. The king drew a deep breath. "Well, that settles it, doesn't it? Corenwald has a champion."

Chapter Twenty

The Champion Prepares

A messenger was dispatched to the enemy camp. He bore a letter accepting Greidawl's challenge. The champion of Corenwald would meet the Pyrthen in the valley between the two camps, at noon the following day.

Word quickly spread among the Corenwalders that a champion had presented himself, but no one seemed to know who he was. The circle of tents in the command yard had been sealed off completely. No one had come into the yard or gone out since the news of the champion first began to spread. There was much speculation regarding the hero's identity. None of the obvious candidates among Corenwald's mightiest warriors had volunteered—that much was well known. The prevailing belief was that the king and his advisers had sent away for a mercenary—a foreign fighter working strictly for pay, not for loyalty to a king or cause. But where would the king find a man who would face certain death for mere money?

For all the interest it generated, however, news of the champion created little hope of deliverance among the Corenwalders. In the Corenwalder imagination, Greidawl was more than a man. As enormous as he was in fact, in their eyes he loomed ten times larger. Day and night, the

Corenwalders meditated on the Pyrthen champion, and in their minds he had become like a god, invulnerable to any human assault.

Aidan, meanwhile, had been given his own little tent within the command yard. There he was supposed to rest in preparation for the next day's battle. But he had little opportunity for rest, for generals and advisers—Darrow's entire inner circle, it seemed—came by in a steady stream to offer strategies and advice for the battle.

None of these men had even entertained the thought of facing Greidawl themselves, but they all had their opinions about how best to defeat him. And their opinions all seemed to disagree with one another.

"The secret is to hit him high. That's the one thing a big man can't defend against."

"The only way to beat a man this big is to hit him low, of course. You've got to cut him down to your own size."

"Keep moving. Never stand still, even for a moment."

"Make sure you stand your ground. You can't really strike if you're on the run."

"You'll want to use a big two-handed sword—the biggest you can lift. It takes a big weapon to hurt an opponent this big."

"You'll need a small sword, obviously, something you can jab and move with. Your only hope is to find a seam in Greidawl's armor."

Aidan's head was swimming with all this contradictory advice when King Darrow's armor bearer arrived to fetch him to the royal armory. Aidan left his tent with the armor bearer, leaving behind two noblemen arguing over the relative merits of chain mail and plate mail.

The large tent that served as the royal armory stood beside the council tent. Its roof flaps were open to the afternoon sun, which gleamed on the burnished steel of the arms and armor within. Just inside the entrance to the armory a dozen suits of armor—six on either side—stood still and straight, as if guarding the place. Behind them were forests of spears and lances propped in wooden racks—row upon row, their polished points flashing in the sun. The sides of the armory tent were hung with shields, each embossed with the golden boar on a field of royal blue, decorated with brass rivets and bands. There were tall, curved shields that a soldier could crouch behind in case of an arrow volley, as well as the small round bucklers more suitable for the close work of foot soldiers and the long oval shields used by cavalrymen. Bundles of blue-feathered arrows were stacked like firewood beside dozens of smooth and narrow longbows.

Aidan had never seen such a complete and varied collection of arms. Of the swords arranged along a table, no two were alike. Heavy two-handed swords were next to long, slender sabers. Short, thick thrusting swords were displayed alongside light but deadly rapiers.

Aidan was admiring the broad curve of a scimitar when King Darrow entered the tent behind him. "Beautiful, isn't it?" he said, gesturing toward the scimitar. "It belonged to a pirate king we captured in a sea battle near Middenmarsh."

"Your Majesty," said Aidan, bowing to the king. He wasn't sure what else to say. He was caught off guard by the king's casual tone.

"You are doing a great service to your king and country," continued the king. "I am grateful to you, and so is all of Corenwald."

Aidan bowed again to his king, not sure what to say. *You're welcome? Don't mention it?*

"Here you have it," Darrow went on, "my entire armory. Arm yourself for tomorrow's battle. You are welcome to anything in here." A surge of excitement electrified Aidan. The place was full of the most fabulous weapons. How would he ever choose?

The king's armor bearer approached, staggering under a pile of steel armor. "You've met Thimble already," said the king. "He has gathered up some armor for you to try on."

Thimble went to work on Aidan. First, he strapped a pair of shin guards around his legs. This took some creativity on Thimble's part because the shin guards were made to fit snugly around calves that were twice the size of Aidan's. Then he buckled on a pair of thigh plates. Aidan's legs were so short, however, that the thigh plates and shin guards overlapped. He couldn't quite straighten his legs and had to walk in a slight squat.

By the time Thimble had strapped the breastplate and backplate on Aidan, the suit of armor was starting to get quite heavy. Aidan looked like a turtle who had borrowed a shell from a much larger turtle, and he was about as mobile as a turtle too. Thimble fitted the throat guard around Aidan's neck, attached arm plates to his shoulders and upper arms, and pulled heavy steel gloves over his hands. Aidan could barely move at all.

When Thimble placed the helmet on Aidan's head and flipped the visor down, Aidan felt like a mule wearing a very heavy set of blinders. He could see what was directly in front of his face but nothing else. "How do you see out of this thing?" he asked. His voice echoed around him as if his head were in a bucket, which, in a way, it was. "How do you breathe?" he asked, with the slightest hint of panic in his voice. He was starting to feel enclosed.

"Outstanding!" said the king, knocking on Aidan's backplate. It made a hollow, metallic echo. "Now you look like a true hero of Corenwald!" Aidan felt ridiculous not heroic.

"Now that your armor is taken care of," continued the king, "let's see about your armaments. Come over here; let me show you some things." Nearly immobilized by his heavy, awkward armor, Aidan creaked and shuffled as best he could toward the sound of the king's voice. With each tiny step he squeaked and clanged like a door on old hinges.

"Against a man in iron armor, blunt force always helps," said the king. "This case is where I keep my melee weapons: maces, clubs, war hammers, flails, battle-axes. Pick something out; see how it feels to you."

The visor made it impossible for Aidan to see what he was doing, but he reached a steel-gloved hand into the weapons box and grabbed the first thing he put his hand on—a thick iron chain. Pulling it out, he found a handle at one end of the chain, and at the other end a heavy iron ball, bigger than a grapefruit, with sharp spikes sticking out in every direction.

"A flail," observed the king. "Very good choice."

Aidan hesitated. He had never seen a flail before and wasn't sure how it worked.

"Just grab the handle," offered the king, placing the handle in Aidan's right hand, "and whip it around so that the ball flies in a circle around your head. Careful, now— don't let it hit you. Hit your opponent with that heavy ball, and he'll know he's been hit." The king took several steps back, giving Aidan plenty of room to swing. "Give it a try; see how it works."

Cautiously at first, Aidan began to swing the flail. Lifting his arm was difficult, but he soon got a feel for the motion, and the spiky, menacing ball was whirring around his head like a massive sling stone. Just as he began to get comfortable with his new weapon, however, the handle slipped out of his gloved hand. The flail ball rocketed through the air, just over the king's head, and tore through the side of the tent. A dozen or more blue-and-gold shields came crashing to the ground with a huge clamor, knocking over the spears that stood in ranks by that side of the tent. A hundred spears and javelins rolled across the floor of the armory tent.

Aidan, meanwhile, had lost his balance, outweighed by his top-heavy armor. He blindly staggered forward, then backward, scattering a stack of pole-axes, then over-turning the table of swords with a tremendous crash before he himself clattered to the ground.

Within seconds ten members of Darrow's royal body-guard had stormed the armory tent, convinced by the sound of things that a full-blown melee had broken out. They laughed uproariously to see that the whole thing was caused by a twelve-year-old boy playing dress-up— a boy who now lay on his back like a beetle, unable to help himself.

Aidan's face burned with humiliation. Two of the guards helped him to his feet, and he immediately pulled the helmet from his head and began unstrapping the other pieces of armor.

"Thank you, Your Majesty, for your kind offer," he said, still breathing heavily, "but I think it will be best if I face the Pyrthen with the weapon I know best, in clothes that don't restrict my freedom to move."

"What weapon?" asked the king, curious.

"A sling. I may be young, but I have years of experience protecting my flocks with nothing more than a sling and staff. I have put wolves and bears to flight. I killed a panther with a single sling stone."

"Frightening a wolf and killing a giant are two very different things!" began the king, with rising voice. "Killing a panther with a sling is an impressive feat, but there is such a thing as a lucky shot. I wouldn't count on doing it again."

"Your Majesty," answered Aidan, still unstrapping, "you have been most generous to me, and I do not wish to seem ungrateful. But the truth is, nothing short of a miracle of the One God could deliver us from the hand of the Pyrthens tomorrow. There is no armor in this armory, and no weapons, that make it possible for a twelve-year-old boy to defeat Greidawl. Only by a miracle can I survive tomorrow's battle, with or without this armor, with or without these weapons.

"If I am defeated tomorrow, I want to die as I have lived—a shepherd boy, with the sun on my forehead and the breeze in my hair. But if I overcome, everyone must know that the One God, and not Aidan Errolson, is the

Champion of Corenwald. Neither arms nor armor can deliver Corenwald—only the arm of the One God."

The king's eyes grew wet with tears as he listened to the shepherd boy. He remembered a time when he, too, lived to serve the true Champion of Corenwald. "Your wish is granted," said the king softly. "Live or die the way you see fit." He put his hand on Aidan's head, the way Aidan's father had done so often, then walked silently from the armory, lost in a memory of Corenwald of old.

✝ ✝ ✝

Aidan spent the rest of the afternoon in solitude. His string of visitors had played out. Sitting alone in his tent, he was assailed by doubts and fears. Whatever made him think he could defeat a giant with a sling? Why was he throwing his life away? For Corenwald? What was Corenwald, anyway? The Corenwalders outside his tent were a bunch of cowards and self-servers who wouldn't know what to do with themselves even if he did manage somehow to deliver them.

Aidan began to consider running away. But where could he run? He couldn't go home, for running away would bring shame to his father and brothers, and he couldn't possibly face them. Perhaps he could join the feechie band in the swamp alongside Bayberry Creek. The feechies would be glad to have him, wouldn't they?

Aidan was so deep in this thought that he didn't notice the two goats nuzzling through the flap into his tent. "Maaahhh," said the nanny, bringing Aidan back to the present. He pulled open his tent flap, and there stood the old prophet, with his piercing green eyes and his big white salad of hair. Aidan gave Bayard an uncertain smile and motioned him into the tent.

The goats sniffed around the tent looking for something to eat while Aidan and Bayard looked at one another, neither saying a word. Bayard saw things other people couldn't see. Did he know the cowardly thoughts that Aidan had just been entertaining?

At last Aidan spoke, unable to stand the silence any longer. "Bayard, am I being a fool?"

Bayard beamed a kindly smile on the boy. "Son of Errol, there are many kinds of fool. Do not ask, 'Am I being a fool?' Ask, 'Am I being the right sort of fool?'"

Aidan shook his head. The old man could never give a straight answer. "How did I get into this mess?" asked Aidan. "I just came to deliver some bread and cheese to my brothers."

"I know you cannot see it now," answered Bayard, "not yet, but this mess is the whole reason you are here. You only *thought* you were here to deliver bread and cheese."

"How about you, Bayard? Why are you here?"

"You might say I've come out of retirement. Never has a king needed a truthspeaker at his side more than Darrow needs one now."

Aidan sniffed. "A lot of good it's done him."

"A truthspeaker can only do so much, young Errolson. Darrow has heard the truth. That is why I am here. Tomorrow he will *see* the truth. That is why you are here."

Bayard snapped his fingers, and his goats hopped over to stand beside him. "Greidawl is a monster. You are right to fear him. Only love goodness more than you fear evil."

Bayard chuckled to himself and shook his head. "He thought he was here to deliver bread and cheese!" he told the billy goat. Then he spoke to Aidan. "Live the life that unfolds before you. The One God is with you."

He turned toward the door. "I have some people to see. I won't be here for tomorrow's battle." He nudged his goats out into the evening. Then, just before ducking through the flap, he turned back to Aidan. "Have you decided yet?"

Aidan looked at the old man, confused. "Decided what?"

"Whether I'm a prophet or a madman."

Chapter Twenty-One

"Remember! Remember!"

Errol Finlayson
Longleaf Manor
Corenwald

Dear Father—

I'm not sure I can explain why I'm doing this, but I imagine it's what you would do if you were here. The first time I met the Truthspeaker, he told me to love goodness more than I fear evil. I kept thinking I had heard that advice somewhere before. It just now dawned on me: I had never heard it before, but every day of my life I had seen it in a father who always, always made sure his sons remembered what sort of God we serve.

I trust I shall see you soon.

Your devoted son,
Aidan

On the day of the combat, at the appointed time of midday, the two armies arrayed themselves along either edge of the valley that separated their two camps. Normally a peaceful little vale, now the place bristled with thousands of spears and pikes, swords and battle-axes.

On the eastern rim the Corenwalders' uniforms formed a wall of blue and gold. Their faces were pale and sickly. Their eyes darted to and fro. They believed themselves to be on the brink of defeat and enslavement. On the western edge of the valley, the grim Pyrthens, in their black armor and spiked helmets, formed a black sea ready to surge over the little valley and the kingdom beyond.

On the valley floor paced Greidawl, the Pyrthens' iron champion. His eyes burned with pent-up rage. He was a killing machine, and yet he had spent more than two weeks on a battle plain with no release for his murderous impulses. No Corenwalder champion had yet presented himself. Greidawl's bloodlust grew as he imagined the destruction he would unleash on the cowards of Corenwald should they fail to deliver a champion. He abruptly stopped his pacing, though, when he saw a boy, unarmed and dressed in the homespun tunic of a country boy, scrambling down the eastern wall of the valley.

A murmur of speculation arose from the Pyrthen side. Was this the armor bearer of the Corenwalder champion?

He wasn't bearing any armor. Was he a messenger boy, bringing a message from the champion of Corenwald to the champion of Pyrth? He did have a side pouch like a messenger boy, but this boy wasn't wearing the hat that messengers usually wore. The Pyrthens, and Greidawl especially, watched the boy as he loped toward the middle of the valley floor.

A few late wildflowers were blooming in the valley. The midday heat had long since overwhelmed the cool of morning. When he had closed half the distance to the Pyrthen, Aidan knelt. He needed sling stones, and he selected five flat, well-balanced ones that had been rubbed smooth by years of flowing water when the river still ran here.

Greidawl turned toward the Pyrthens behind him. "Look!" he boomed, pointing at the kneeling form of the boy at the brook, "the boy is praying! Ha! He'd better pray!" He turned to the Corenwalders. "You all had better pray!" He laughed at the Corenwalders, and the Pyrthens laughed, too, bowing and waving their hands in mock prayers.

Aidan placed the five smooth stones in his side pouch, where he kept his sling. Then he rose and walked with slow, sure steps toward Greidawl. His gaze was steady, his face a picture of pure calm. The Pyrthen was confused and a little agitated by the boy's actions. He was still waiting for a mighty man of Corenwald to appear.

"Who are you, boy?" he snarled. "Where is the champion of Corenwald?"

"The Champion of Corenwald is here already," answered Aidan. "You stand before him now."

Greidawl looked at Aidan with some annoyance. "You are no champion. You aren't even a man." He looked scornfully at Aidan's skinny frame. "You're hardly even a boy! Look at you—you're a stick."

Undaunted by Greidawl's scorn, Aidan met his gaze. The Pyrthen was furious. He raised his spear and pointed it at King Darrow, who watched the scene from the edge of the valley. "Am I a dog," he roared, "that you should come at me with a stick?" He was shaking with rage. "Send a champion to face me!"

"Corenwald has a Champion," said Aidan firmly. "He is the One God."

"The One God?" Greidawl mocked. He laughed cruelly and pointed his spear at Aidan. "Could the One God do no better than you?"

Aidan stood with his hands on his hips, his feet apart. "The One God can deliver me. But even if he doesn't deliver me, I still won't bow down to you or any other Pyrthen."

Greidawl laughed again. He looked past Aidan to the Corenwalders on the valley's edge. "I see no God. I hear no God. I feel no God." He raised his massive spear. In his gigantic hand it seemed no bigger than a shepherd's staff. "But this—*this* is real. Twenty-five pounds of ashwood and iron. What do you suppose your 'One God' can do about this?"

With a quickness that seemed impossible for such a huge man, the Pyrthen hurled the spear at Aidan the way a normal man would toss a dart. A cheer erupted from the Pyrthen side of the valley as the massive spear careered toward the shepherd boy. Greidawl's aim was sure: he could hardly miss his target at such close range. Nor could anyone hope to dodge a spear thrown with such suddenness and velocity. Aidan didn't flinch. The iron spearhead—heavier than his own head, heavy enough to spill his life in an instant—whistled past, only inches from his ear. The spear stuck in the clay ten paces behind him, its ashwood shaft still quivering from the force of Greidawl's mighty heave.

The Pyrthens' cheer died on their lips. On the Corenwalder side, terror gave way to relief, but hope was still far away. Aidan smiled an unworried little smile at the enraged Pyrthen. "Are ashwood and iron more real than the living God? Who buried the iron in the ribs of the earth? Who makes the ashwood to grow upon the hill?"

Aidan reached in his side pouch for his sling and one of the smooth stones he had picked up. He swung the slingstone over his head with a free looping motion, as if he were slinging at targets in the bottom pasture. "And the One God," Aidan continued, "has given you into my hands."

Aidan's nonchalance was too much for Greidawl to bear. He reached for his battle-ax, a ridiculously large and heavy iron thing, as wide across as Aidan's shoulders. Raising the ax above his head, he bellowed like a bull in its fury, then charged Aidan with all the speed his iron armor and lumbering size would allow.

The lazy loops of Aidan's sling tightened into whipping circles as the champion of Pyrth bore down. The earth shook with each ironclad footfall. But Aidan stood firm and waited for Greidawl to bring himself into range.

The stone whizzed in a circle around Aidan's head, and the roaring Pyrthen came on. He was determined to split Aidan in two, the way a farmer splits a log. He got so close that Aidan could see the curling hairs in Greidawl's nose. Aidan could almost feel the stinking heat of the great warrior's breath. The looming Pyrthen filled Aidan's frame of vision, making a target so large that Aidan could hardly miss him. At last, the shepherd boy let fly.

Greidawl was reaching back with his battle-ax, poised to deliver an obliterating blow to the insolent little Corenwalder, when the stone struck him. Embedding in his forehead, the flat stone jutted out over his one black eyebrow like a little shelf. He staggered back one step, forward two steps, then back another step. His eyelids fluttered. His arms went limp, and the ax fell with a heavy thud behind him. He crumpled down on himself, and with a crash like a dozen iron kettles dropped from a rooftop, he fell forward, his head at Aidan's feet.

But Aidan's work wasn't done. Greidawl was senseless not dead. With both hands Aidan laid hold of the battle-ax and dragged it the seven feet from the great Pyrthen's feet to his head. The ax weighed nearly as much as Aidan did, and he prayed he would be able to heft it before Greidawl came to his senses. He had never wielded a battle-ax before, but he had driven many a post with a heavy iron sledge. The practice served him well. He squared his feet to Greidawl's fallen form, centering on the patch of bare neck left unprotected by the skewed helmet. With a groaning effort, he raised the ax, staggering under its massive weight.

The ax hung in the air. Here was the future of Corenwald, fifty pounds of iron balanced precariously over the head of a shepherd boy. Would it fall backward, toppling the boy and the kingdom with it? Or would it fall forward to end the terror that had so enslaved the imaginations of Corenwald's fighting men? Aidan struggled to balance the ax, which now seemed determined not to strike a blow against its Pyrthen master.

Greidawl's huge fingers began to move, then his arms. He was trying to raise himself. Seeing his enemy stir, Aidan summoned his last reserves of strength. As he tipped the ax forward, he made the valley echo with a shout such as no Pyrthen, and very few Corenwalders, had ever heard before: *"Haawweee!"*

Greidawl was just beginning to regain consciousness. He groggily turned his head toward the shepherd boy's shout. The last thing he ever saw was his own battle-ax plunging down on him like a thunderstroke.

The Pyrthens on the western bank stood in shocked silence. They never thought they would see their champion slain. The Corenwalders were silent, too, but only for a moment. They quickly erupted in wild whoops and shouts and hoots of joy and relief. Turning to face his countrymen, Aidan lifted Greidawl's helmet in salute to the fighting men of Corenwald. The Corenwalders cheered all the more, then they grew quiet again when it became clear that their young champion had something to say to them.

Aidan's victory speech was short—only two words, in fact. But those two words echoed across the Bonifay Plain and throughout Corenwalder history: "Remember! Remember!"

The Corenwalders did remember. They remembered the One God who had delivered them from the Pyrthens so many times before, who was even now delivering them. They remembered what it meant to be "Corenwalders free and true." They remembered that they were brave men and mighty warriors. They remembered why the great empire so hated the free Corenwalders.

Greidawl, while he lived, had been like a heavy fog descended on the Corenwalders. When they looked about them, they couldn't see the world as it was, only the fog. But now Greidawl was dead, and it was as if the fog had been burned away by the bright light of day. The Corenwalders could see again, and the world they saw was even more beautiful than they had remembered. They, and not the Pyrthens, were the masters of their island kingdom. According to the terms of Greidawl's challenge, and thanks to the bravery of a shepherd boy and the providence of the One God, the invaders were now their slaves.

Aidan surveyed his countrymen. They weren't the same men he had seen only an hour before. Gone were the hangdog looks and the sour faces of defeated men. They stood straighter now. The glint of the sun on their weapons was now matched by a glint of confidence in the warriors' eyes. They looked like Corenwalders. *That's all they needed,* thought Aidan. *To remember.* He remembered the Wilderking Chant:

He will silence the braggart,
ennoble the coward.
Watch for the Wilderking!

Chapter Twenty-Two

Thunder

Aidan was drifting into a pleasant reverie of the Corenwald of old when he heard a strange sort of music from the Pyrthen line behind him—three *twangs*, pitched a little lower than the low string on a lute—*twang-twa-twang*—so rapid as to be nearly simultaneous. Black-feathered arrows whistled past, one just inches from his left ear, one over his head. A third arrow grazed his right arm just below the shoulder. He instinctively dropped to the ground. Four more twangs; four black-feathered arrows sailed over him, right where he had stood a second earlier.

He quickly took cover behind the ironclad hulk of Greidawl's lifeless body. The strange music, he realized, was the twang of Pyrthen bowstrings. Aidan crouched as low as he could; arrows continued to whistle just over his head or deflect off the iron plates of Greidawl's armor.

Then a hail of blue-feathered arrows came flying over from the Corenwalders' side of the valley. On the Pyrthen side, five archers fell. The battle was on. Before Aidan knew what was happening, foot soldiers from both sides were spilling into the valley and charging toward one another. The armies collided in two long lines along the middle of the valley, and Aidan found himself in the midst of ferocious fighting.

Lacking either arms or armor, Aidan thought it best to lie low. His arm was streaked with the blood trickling from the wound left by the grazing arrow. He improved his defensive position behind Greidawl's bulk by pulling the huge shield over himself, making an iron lean-to where he was hidden and a little safer. He realized there was little he could do but wait it out. The hacking and jabbing were terrible to see. The pounding of swords and axes on shields, the screams and groans of wounded men were awful to hear.

A hand grabbed the edge of the iron shield and flipped it over. His covering gone, Aidan was as exposed and vulnerable as a cockroach when a boy turns over a log. He almost wept with relief and gratitude when he realized that it wasn't a Pyrthen who had uncovered him but his brother Brennus.

"Now look what you've done!" said Brennus with mock sternness. He was smiling. "You've saved Corenwald. That's what." He motioned to Percy, Jasper, and Maynard, who were also searching for their little brother among the chaos of the battle. They formed a guard around Brennus and Aidan.

"You're bleeding," observed Brennus. "How bad is it?"

"Not bad at all," Aidan assured him. "But still, I wouldn't mind getting out of here."

"You'll be back in the camp in no time."

Maynard, Jasper, and Percy formed a rear guard. Brennus put a protective arm around Aidan, and they made for the Corenwalder camp. As they ran, Brennus leaned in toward Aidan's ear and said something that astonished his little brother: "Hail to the Wilderking!"

Though Aidan insisted he was fine, the brothers deposited him at the surgeon's tent to have his wound treated. Then they returned to the battle.

The surgeon, an old man with a white mustache and wet blue eyes, dabbed at Aidan's bloodied arm. "Just a flesh wound," he observed. "Not much more than a nick."

He reached for a jar of turpentine gum. "This is going to burn a bit," he warned, "but it will seal you up nicely—and keep the termites out!" He laughed at his own joke. "There," he said as he coated the wound, "good as new."

The surgeon was wrapping Aidan's upper arm with cotton strips when he noticed the feechiemark on his forearm. "What happened there?" he asked.

"That?" answered Aidan, a little startled. "That's a . . . that's a . . ." He decided it would be better not to get specific. "That's a burn scar."

"It almost looks like an alligator," the surgeon remarked. "Look, there's the mouth; there's the tail curving around." A look of remembrance lit the old surgeon's face. "I once saw a scar like this one on the forearm of a man I was treating."

Aidan's eyes grew wide. The man the surgeon spoke of must have been a feechiefriend. "Who was it?" he asked eagerly.

"Oh, heavens, I couldn't possibly remember. It must have been forty years ago. I was still a surgeon's apprentice." He smiled wistfully to think about those days. "And besides, it was in the middle of a very hot battle.

I've forgotten the man—if, indeed, I ever knew him—but a scar like that is hard to forget."

The din of battle resounded outside the surgeon's tent. "But there are Corenwalders lying hurt on the field even now. I must go to them." He began making preparations to leave.

"You've made us all proud to be Corenwalders, young Errolson," the old man announced.

Aidan smiled at him. "Corenwalders free and true."

"Hear, hear," the surgeon answered. "I'll leave you here to rest. You need it. Just stay here, and I'll be back to check on you when I can." He gathered up the last few things into his surgeon's bag and left for the battlefield.

Aidan lay back on his cot and wondered for a minute about the mysterious feechiefriend that the old man had met so many years before. But only for a minute. Aidan had no intention of lying in a tent while his brothers and countrymen battled an invading army.

The camp was more or less deserted, so he walked to the armory and helped himself to a small sword and buckler. Then he hurried out to the battle, sword raised, mouth stretched with a primal shout of exuberance.

By the time Aidan got to the battle valley, his country-men had pushed the skirmish line all the way back to the slope leading up to the Pyrthen camp. At last, thought Aidan, they look like the mighty men of Corenwald, riding fast and striking hard in defense of their island. But it is no easy matter to fight uphill, even for men who, like the Corenwalders, have just rediscovered strength they forgot they had. Fighting downhill, the Pyrthens, with their superior numbers, were able to hold their line at the edge of their encampment. They dug in, and the Corenwalders were unable to get the momentum to push up out of the valley floor and overrun them. The Corenwalder line was stretching thin.

By the time Aidan caught up to the rear guard, King Darrow realized that his army had to fall back and regroup before it could take the Pyrthen camp. The retreat flags went up, and the Corenwalders began to withdraw eastward toward their own encampment. The Pyrthens didn't pursue. They had had all they wanted of the Corenwalders that day; they seemed content to lick their wounds and wait for the next day's fighting.

Aidan had fallen in with a cluster of soldiers from the Tambluff Regiment when a crack of thunder split the air above him. Striking the earth about fifty strides ahead of him, the thunderbolt sent earth and men flying through the air. Aidan looked to the sky. It was cloudless. Another clap of thunder was followed by another shower of earth. A third flattened two tents in the Corenwalder camp.

Behind him, from the Pyrthen camp, Aidan heard taunting cheers. He turned to see what was happening, and through a film of white smoke he could see that the Pyrthen foot soldiers had withdrawn from the valley's edge to make way for three heavy carriages. Laid across each carriage was a huge tube of black iron, as big around as a saw log and almost as long, pointed toward the Corenwalders. A cluster of Pyrthens worked busily around the near end of each tube—though Aidan couldn't see what they were doing. Then one of the soldiers poked what appeared to be a mop into the tube and jabbed it around a few times, and a soldier with an officer's plume touched the other end of the tube with a lit pine knot.

Then the thunder came again. A flash of white fire shot out of the tube's open end. A high whistle soared over Aidan's head, and behind him, nearly at the Corenwalder edge of the valley, came the earth-shattering crash and the screams of men thrown skyward by the impact.

The Pyrthens, Aidan realized, had figured out how to make thunder in those iron tubes. And mule teams were pulling three more into position. Aidan joined the throng that was now running panic-stricken from the enemy they were so thoroughly defeating only a half-hour before.

The camp offered little protection. The Pyrthens could easily throw thunder clear across the valley. The only good news was that the Pyrthens, though they knew how to make thunder, weren't very good at making it go where they wanted. The great majority of thunderbolts landed in the valley short of the Corenwalder camp or in the open plain beyond.

Nevertheless, the camp was in an uproar. The thunderbolts that did find their way into the camp did considerable damage, and the shaking of the earth and the deafening noise shattered the Corenwalders' nerves. By now, they could barely see the Pyrthens for the curtain of white smoke that issued from the thunder-tubes. They mostly saw the bright flash of the thunder-fire. The sweet, acrid smoke, carried across the valley by a westerly breeze, burned their eyes and noses.

In the confusion, Aidan was unable to find his brothers' tent, so he picked his way through his thunderstruck countrymen to the command yard. That was, after all, where his tent was. The guards recognized him and saluted as he passed their checkpoint.

Inside the command yard, King Darrow and half a dozen noblemen were circled around a crater where one of the thunderbolts had come to earth. Lord Grady was tapping his walking stick on something smooth and metallic at the bottom of the crater. It was the top half of a big iron ball, a little smaller than a cantaloupe.

"It's not thunderbolts they're throwing at us," Lord Grady observed. "It's these iron balls."

Another deafening explosion shook the earth not twenty strides away. "They might as well be thunderbolts," Selwyn remarked grimly, "for all our ability to defend against them."

"Oh, the fiendish imagination of the Pyrthen!" groaned Lord Radnor. "To rain down destruction from half a league away!"

King Darrow had been deep in thought this whole time, pondering his options, racking his brain for a plan that would get them out of this predicament. Now he spoke: "That's enough poor-mouthing. We haven't come here to lose this battle. The One God is with us." He looked at Aidan. "Young Errolson showed us that. If we despair, our men will despair. And Corenwald will be lost."

Another thunder-ball whistled overhead and flattened a tent four rows over. "We mustn't despair," the king repeated, more to himself than to anyone else.

Just then two soldiers approached. One wore an officer's uniform; the second was an older foot soldier—too old, really, to be a foot soldier—who had the earthy, sunburned look of a farmer. They both saluted King Darrow. "Your Majesty," began the officer, "I am Captain Perrin of the Bluemoss Regiment. This is Harlan Ebbetson, one of the soldiers under my command. He has information you may find useful."

The king addressed the foot soldier: "Speak, Harlan. Your king listens."

The soldier removed his helmet to address the king, but when the earth shook again with the impact of a distant thunder-ball, he thought better of it and put it back on with a sheepish nod to Darrow. "Your Majesty," he began in the slow drawl of the Middle Shires, "when I was a boy, my family farmed this land. Our house stood hard by that big live oak where the giant stands—" he caught himself and nodded toward Aidan, "—used to stand to taunt us every day. The house is gone now. The Pyrthens burned it to the ground in the first invasion, and we moved away to Bluemoss."

Another Pyrthen thunder-ball shattered the air. When the noise subsided, Harlan continued. "About fifty strides beyond that oak tree, there's an underground cave, just a hole in the ground. We used to store cheese and eggs and smoked meat there in the coolness." Amid the chaos of battle, the old farmer's slow, meandering way of telling the story was maddening. The noblemen grew fidgety.

Harlan pointed north. "And up this way, about a half-hour's walk, there's another cave."

Selwyn spoke impatiently. "Enough preliminaries! What's your information?"

Harlan blinked at the nobleman, then blinked again. "Well, sir," he drawled, "that *was* the information."

The captain broke in to explain. "The point is, the two caves might connect underground—like a secret passageway."

Kink Darrow was starting to get the idea. "So we might be able to send a troop of soldiers into the very heart of the enemy camp—"

"Right," answered the captain, visibly excited by the prospect.

"And who knows what havoc they could wreak," added Radnor.

The captain nodded his head eagerly. "That's what I was thinking."

"Perhaps they could capture the Pyrthen thundertubes," suggested Lord Halbard.

"If they were part of a larger assault, maybe so," the king remarked. He spoke to Harlan. "So what are the chances that these two caves connect?"

"Oh, I'd say there's a pretty decent chance," answered the farmer-soldier. The growing excitement among the noblemen was palpable. "But that ain't the problem," he added.

"Not the problem?" huffed Lord Selwyn. "Then what *is* the problem?"

"The problem's finding the way. When that limestone melts away to make a cave, it can leave a maze of tunnels and twisting pathways about like an ant bed." This news dampened the group's spirits. Harlan went on. "Then there's a good chance the path you're looking for is underwater. Cousin of mine drowned in a cave like that."

He paused a few seconds out of respect for his cousin. "And dark!" he continued. "Man, you never seen such darkness. No such thing as daytime in a cave!" He shivered to think of his last expedition underground, more than thirty years earlier, before the first western invasion. "Low ceilings, tight squeezes, sore back, bruised knees— I don't ever want to go in a cave again."

King Darrow and his advisers were dejected now. Their hopes of finding a secret tunnel to the Pyrthens were all but crushed.

"But then again," Harlan added cheerfully, "you might get down there and find it's a straight shot from here to there. You never know in a cave."

"So to summarize," sighed Selwyn, "there's a chance that there's an underground path from our side of the valley to the Pyrthen camp. There's a chance it isn't underwater. There's a chance this path won't have places too narrow for armed soldiers to pass through. There's a chance we'll be able to find this path. And there's a chance that if a troop of soldiers actually made it to the Pyrthen camp, they'd be able to do us any good."

Harlan nodded. "Sounds about right."

"That adds up to a very slim chance this scheme could work," moaned Selwyn.

"True," answered King Darrow, "but these are desperate times. We must try it." He began pacing back and forth, thinking how best to make this happen. "There's no point in sending a troop of armed soldiers and hoping they find their way," he began. "We'll send a team of scouts to explore the caves and mark a path, if there is one, for the soldiers to follow."

"How about miners?" Aidan suggested. "Our regular scouts' skill and training won't do them much good underground. But miners spend their days inside the earth."

"The boy's right," agreed Lord Grady. "The mines of Greasy Cave are in my shire. Shall we send for some Greasy Cave boys?"

"Yes," answered the king. "Grady, go to the captain of their regiment. Tell him to muster a team of five experienced miners for a special mission—a mission that might save their kingdom."

Then the king added, under his breath, "An all-important, near-impossible mission."

Aidan broke the uncomfortable silence that followed. "Er . . . Your Majesty? . . . Could I go with the troop of miner-scouts?"

The king shook his head. "Young Errolson, you've risked your life enough today."

"But, Sire," Aidan insisted, "don't you think someone small should be in the party?"

Harlan chimed in, "There's some mighty tight spots in a cave."

"And the miners I know," added Aidan, "are pretty broad about the chest and shoulders."

The king thought on this. "You may be right, Errolson. The miner-scouts might need someone who has the body of a boy but the wits of a man."

Chapter Twenty-Three

The Miner-Scouts

The leader of the miner-scouts was Gustus, the eldest of the company and their foreman at the mines of Greasy Cave. His thick beard was turning gray, but he was still a man of tremendous strength and vitality. His gruff way of talking didn't disguise the tenderness he felt toward his men or his commitment to their well-being. Of the four other miner-scouts, three—Cedric, Ernest, and Clayton—were all made from the same mold as Gustus. They were short, burly men, accustomed to the perils and difficulties of working below the earth.

One of the miners, however, was different from the others. Arliss was a teenager, only three or four years older than Aidan. He was tall and lanky and didn't much look like a miner. He hadn't yet grown into his full strength, so he lacked the other miners' skill with pickax and shovel. Nevertheless, he had a vital part to play in the mission.

Gustus had selected Arliss for the company because he had what people around Greasy Cave called "the miner's head." In the sheer blackness of the underground, it is a rare person who can maintain a sense of place and time. In an unfamiliar mine, or a mine that was not properly marked, even a miner with many years' experience could get turned around and find himself lost for days. But Arliss, like his father and his father before him, had an uncanny ability to navigate underground. Without sun or stars to guide him, he could always find true north. Without reference to horizon or landmark, he could always judge how far he had traveled. Arliss lacked the experience of the other miner-scouts, but, as Gustus was well aware, they were headed to a place where nobody had any experience. At some point, they would have to rely on instinct and intuition. They would have to rely on the miner's head.

Aidan rounded out the group. His chief contribution was his small size. Should the way get too narrow for the miners to pass, it would be Aidan's job to scout ahead. Otherwise, the young hero would mostly trail along with the group and try to stay out of the way.

The moon had not yet risen when the miner-scouts lit out for the cave entrance on the Corenwalder side of the valley. The night sky was clear, and the stars provided only enough light for the little troop to pick its way through the wiregrass. They all wore oaken miner's helmets, and each carried a rope and climbing hook, a pack with hardtack biscuit, a tinderbox for lighting fires, a few basic supplies, a water bladder, and a bundle of seven torches made of river cane and pine pitch.

Each of the miners, as always, had a pickax and shovel strapped to his back. Even aboveground, the miners pitched forward when they walked, as if they were in a low tunnel. They had orders not to talk above a whisper until they were underground, so as to avoid the notice of any Pyrthen patrols that might be in the area. But the miners were a talkative bunch. In the dark and gloomy holes where they spent their days, a constant stream of chatter and argument kept their spirits up. They couldn't help talking now.

"Hey, Gustus," called Clayton, "tell me again how we're going to find a hole in the ground on a wide plain in the dark of night."

"Harlan said to look for two big cedars growing so close together they look like two branches of one big tree," answered Gustus, "about a half-hour's walk to the northeast of the camp. He says the cave hole is ten or fifteen strides to the east of the trees."

"And how long has it been since he's seen this cave hole?" asked Cedric.

"Well, let's see . . ." Gustus was figuring. "He said they quit this country after the first western invasion and he hasn't been back since, so what's that, thirty years or more?"

"Hey, Gustus?" It was Clayton again. "How do we know the cave hole on this side leads to the cave hole on the Pyrthen side?"

"We don't know for sure," said Gustus.

"Well, if anybody can find a path underground, it's us," answered Cedric, a little defensively. "We were made for this sort of thing."

"True," said Gustus. "But even so, the caves and tunnels we're used to were dug by human hands. We got maps. We got long experience.

"But these caves," he jabbed his finger toward the ground for emphasis, "these caves were hollowed out by the earth itself—by seeping water that melts away rock like spun sugar. The tunnels of a limestone cave don't give up their secrets very easy. Anybody who goes down that hole, boys, better have a good reason for it."

The company walked on in silence, chewing on what the foreman had said. Ernest was the first to break the silence. "Am I the only one who's not sure this is a good idea?" Nobody answered, so he continued. "I came here to fight Pyrthens, not to get lost in a cave and starve to a skeleton. Appears to me, Corenwald needs all the fighting men it can muster."

Ernest's remarks were met with a general mumble of agreement. But above the mumble came the boyish voice of Arliss, the youngest of the miners. "You're looking at it all wrong." He quickened his step to catch up to Ernest. "Sure, we came to fight, but the truth is, none of us is any great shakes when it comes to soldiering. We're all of us handier with a pickax than a battle-ax."

"What're you saying, Arliss?" grumbled Clayton.

"I'm just saying, it might be that all the days we've spent in the mines were just getting us ready for this day. There's a whole lot we don't know about this mission. We don't know if the cave is passable; we don't know if it goes all the way to the Pyrthen side; we don't know if we can find the way even if it does. But we do know that, whatever this mission turns out to be, there's nobody readier for it than we are."

"Live the life that unfolds before you." It was the first thing Aidan had said since they left camp.

Everyone turned toward Aidan. "What's that, son?" asked Gustus.

"Who knows what the future holds? Only the One

God," explained Aidan. "You just live the little bit of life that you can see in front of you. You live it well. And that gets you ready for whatever unfolds next.

"Yesterday you were miners. Today, you're scouts. Who knows, this might be a big waste of time—or worse. But maybe you're the men who will deliver Corenwald from the Pyrthens. And the brave miners of Greasy Cave will be remembered forever in story and song as the heroes of the Bonifay Plain, whose bravery brought an end to the fifth western invasion." He broke into an impromptu song:

> Oh, the miners brave of Greasy Cave,
> They did not think it odd
> To make their way beneath the clay
> Where human foot has never trod.
> Fol de rol de rol de fol de rol de rol
> De fol de rol de fiddely fol de rol.

> Oh, the miners brave of Greasy Cave,
> Came out the other side.
> They braved the gloom, they challenged doom,
> They made an end to Pyrthen pride.
> Fol de rol de rol de fol de rol de rol
> De fol de rol de fiddely fol de rol.

The miners were unaccustomed to being spoken of as heroes. They rather liked it. Without their even realizing it, their shuffling steps locked into a soldierly march as they sang the refrain from Aidan's song:

> Fol de rol de rol de fol de rol de rol
> De fol de rol de fiddely fol de rol.

Gustus stopped short. "The twin cedars," he said excitedly, pointing ahead. About a hundred strides away, Aidan could just make out the silhouette of the big, bushy trees. The company quickened their pace to keep up with their foreman.

Standing to the east of the cedars, Gustus scanned the landscape in front of him, but he saw no cave entrance. "Ten or fifteen strides to the east of the twin cedars," he said to nobody in particular. "That's what Harlan said. About where that clump of bushes is."

Aidan's heart sank. "Are you sure these are the right trees?"

"Have to be," answered Gustus. "There aren't many trees on this plain, much less big twin cedars. But how can a cave just disappear?"

Arliss, meanwhile, had gone over to the clump of bushes where Gustus had said the cave entrance should be. He was poking at the ground with the handle of his shovel. "Boys," he called, "what you reckon this is?"

Running to where Arliss stood, Aidan could see that the bushes concealed a slight depression in the landscape. The miners circled around Arliss to see what he was poking at in the sand.

"Looks like a rabbit hole to me," offered Clayton.

"Little big for a rabbit hole, ain't it?"

"Well, it ain't no cave entrance, if that's what you're getting at."

"I don't know," Arliss answered, jabbing at the hole with the digging end of his shovel. "I think it's a cave-in." The hole opened a little under the shovel blade.

Encouraged, Arliss attacked the sandy soil with renewed vigor. "Fall to, boys!" he called.

The circle of miners pulled out picks and shovels and went at the hole in the ground, uprooting bushes and sending sand flying. In a matter of seconds, the hole grew to the size of a wagon wheel, gaping like a black mouth in the white sand.

"It's a cave, all right!" shouted Gustus. "It's a cave, boys!" The mission was on in earnest now, and Gustus took charge. "Clayton, Ernest," he ordered, "get a climbing rope ready. Tie off on those cedars."

He put a big, meaty hand on Arliss's bony shoulder. "Arliss, you'll be the first one down the rabbit hole."

Aidan stayed out of the way as the miners made their preparations. Meanwhile, Gustus shuttled back and forth between the cedars and the hole, checking knots, securing packs, encouraging his men. The miners laughed as their foreman sang Aidan's song in his gruff, tuneless way:

Oh, the miners brave of Greasy Cave,
They did not think it odd
To make their way beneath the clay
Where human foot has never trod.
Fol de rol de rol de fol de rol de rol
De fol de rol de fiddely fol de rol.

The rope securely tied, Gustus gathered his men in a circle. "Strap helmets," he ordered, strapping his own as he said it. "Kneepads on." To each of his men he handed two bulky squares of stitched leather stuffed with cotton, which they strapped around their knees.

Gustus threw the free end of the climbing rope down the cave hole. "And now," he said, "to the One God we commend our lives and this mission." He turned to Arliss and gestured toward the cave. "Arliss, lead the way."

The young miner grasped the rope with both hands and backed into the hole. The blackness swallowed his lanky body. Looking up into the starlight, Arliss spoke one last time before he was completely lost in the shadows: "For God! For king! For Corenwald!"

Chapter Twenty-Four

Down a Hole

The company of miners peered into the blackness of the cave hole and strained to hear anything that might tell them how Arliss was doing. It seemed an age before they heard his voice echoing up from the depths: "Bottom-tom-tom-om!"

Aidan went next. Backing hand over hand down the rope, he soon lost sight of the winking starlight and found himself in absolute darkness. It was comfortably cool down the hole; the muggy warmth of the summer night didn't penetrate below the surface. Neither did the smells of the green world make their way into the cave. Above ground, the leafy odors of grass and shrub, the faint perfumes of flower and berry were so constant that Aidan rarely even realized he was breathing them. But down the cave hole, he smelled nothing but muddy clay.

The entry tunnel wasn't a straight drop but rather a step slope leading down to the innards of the earth. The limestone offered poor footing. Aidan hugged the climbing rope tightly as he inched through the narrow chute.

The miners above made no noise. Nor was there any noise from below. Aidan could hear only his own short breaths and the pounding of blood in his temples. Of all his five senses, only the sense of touch was left to him, so he was very aware of the textures around him. In places, the limestone was as smooth as wavy glass and just as slippery. In others, it was as rough as embedded gravel, and sliding over it was a misery. Twice he bumped his head on protruding rocks that would have surely left nasty gashes had he not been wearing his miner's helmet.

At last, Aidan heard a noise below him.

Tchk . . . tchk . . . tchk.

"Arliss?" he called tentatively. "Is that you?"

"It's me," came back Arliss's echoing voice. To Aidan's relief, it didn't sound very far away.

Tchk . . . tchk . . . tchk.

"Trying to strike a fire," Arliss remarked, "but it's mighty damp down here."

Aidan was out of the entry tunnel now and able to stand up straight. He called back up the chute, "Bottom-tom-tom-om." The slightest sound echoed all around the chamber where he now stood.

"Welcome to the underworld," chuckled Arliss in the pitch blackness. "Have a look around."

Tchk . . . tchk . . . tchk.

A few strides away, Aidan saw three sparks in succession. He heard Arliss grumbling in frustration. He stepped carefully toward the sparks, hoping not to stumble on an upthrust rock or break his nose on a hanging stalactite.

Tchk . . . tchk . . . tchk.

At last the spark caught on a little pile of dry tinder and became a tiny, licking flame. Aidan saw the knuckly silhouette of Arliss's hand reach toward the flame with a splinter of fat lighter, which burst into a yellow blaze.

The dim light illuminated a smile of relief and satisfaction on the young miner's narrow face. He took up one of the cane torches at his feet and dropped the flaming splinter among the shaggy fibers at the top. They quickly caught, and the hot-burning pine pitch popped and snapped. He handed the lit torch to Aidan and held out the second torch to borrow fire from Aidan's.

Their eyes had grown accustomed to total darkness, so even the muted light cast by the torches seemed bright. But soon their eyes adjusted, and the boys were astonished to see what sort of cave they were in.

It was an enormous chamber, much bigger than King Darrow's great hall. The walls, floor, and ceiling were carved out of glittering white limestone. Great swaths of golden brown and burnt-red rock seemed to move across the walls like cloud formations. The floor of the cave sloped down to an underground lake, where the water was so clear that the stone below the surface was no less visible than the stone at the water's edge. But where the water grew deep—as deep as any ocean, by the looks of it—it took on a greenish-blue hue.

Aidan and Arliss stood wordlessly, trying to take in the scene before them. Behind them they heard a grunt, and two boots appeared at the end of the entry chute, followed by the legs, the thick round body, and the head and arms of Ernest. He stood blinking in the torchlight, rubbing a banged elbow and stretching a sore backbone. When his eyes adjusted, he staggered back a step, amazed at the scene. "Good heavens!" he exclaimed, and his voice echoed around the chamber. "To think such a world as this was right below our feet, and we never knew it!"

The three remaining miners appeared in their turns, with Gustus bringing up the rear. Each was as awestruck as the others, but each also understood that the beauty of the place didn't lessen its danger.

"All right, boys," began Gustus, "we got a wet cave. That means we got to be very careful of our fire. If we lose fire, we don't get out of this cave alive." He looked intently into the faces of his men. "You saw how dark it was in that entry chute. Without these torches, this whole cave would be just as dark. We can't lose fire," he repeated slowly and emphatically.

"Everybody's got seven torches. That's forty-two torches between us, minus the pair that's already lit, makes forty. That's twenty pair: ten for the trip out, ten for the trip back."

He paused. He wanted to be sure everybody heard him: "When ten pair of torches are burned, we turn for home."

"But, Gustus," interrupted Arliss, "what if we haven't made it to the other side yet?"

"I don't care. I don't care if we haven't made it out of this entry chamber yet. I don't care if we're so close we can smell Pyrthens," answered Gustus. "When we light the eleventh pair of torches, we turn it around. It don't serve any purpose for us to die in a hole for lack of fire to get out." Arliss saw the logic in this. He submitted to his foreman.

"A torch burns three-quarters of an hour," continued Gustus. "That gives us about seven hours to find the Pyrthen camp. So let's move it. The torches are burning."

Taking Aidan's torch, Gustus led the way along the

edge of the lake. He, Ernest, and Cedric formed a trio, and behind them Arliss and Aidan walked in the light of Clayton's torch. It was a relatively easy hike at first, but the lakeside path was not straight. The lake wound its way beneath the earth like a great tunneling snake, and Aidan quickly lost all sense of direction.

"Are we sure we're headed the right way?" he whispered to Arliss.

"Let's hope the path takes a left-hand turn," Arliss whispered back. "We're tracking just a little north of due west."

"No sun, no stars," Aidan observed, "I don't see how you can tell."

Arliss tapped his helmet. "Miner's head. Pap had it. Grandpap had it. I got it too."

The underground landscape—as much as they could see anyway—changed constantly. In places, the lake disappeared completely, dropping away to an even deeper tunnel than the one they were passing through. In places, fields of massive stalagmites stood like whole forests of cypress knees, broad at the base and tapering toward the top. Where the ceiling was lower, they got a good look at the stalactites hanging ponderously over their heads.

All around them echoed the *drip . . . drip . . . drip* of seeping groundwater, heavy with dissolved limestone. It dropped from the bottoms of stalactites to the tops of the stalagmites below, leaving one more molecule of limestone on the tip of each, growing them toward each other in the slow way of underground things. In places the stalactites and stalagmites met to form great pillars from floor to ceiling, monuments to the patient work of water and limestone. In other places, the ceiling was thickly covered with thin, hollow formations like drinking straws. A droplet of water hung from each, and they shone like jewels in the torchlight.

The walls, too, were infinitely varied in color and texture, now white and smooth as alabaster, now striped red and white like bacon, now gray and muddy. The ground they walked on was sometimes smooth and slick, sometimes crunchy with bits of deposited limestone. But mostly it was mud they walked on—or through: slippery mud, sticky mud, ankle-deep in places, in some places even deeper, threatening to take a boot and keep it.

For the first two hours of the trip, the way was broad and the ceilings high enough that the company could walk upright. Though their way was winding, it wasn't a maze. There had been only one path. They appeared to be making good time, and their spirits were high. As a bird flies, it wasn't more than half a league from the east entrance of the cave, where they came in, to the entrance on the Pyrthen side.

"We can't be far now," remarked Ernest. "We're on our third pair of torches, and we've been walking steady this whole time."

After a brief hesitation, Arliss spoke up. "We're not as close as you think. We've been walking due north the last half-hour."

"Due north?" snorted Clayton, "what makes you say that?"

Arliss tapped his helmet.

Gustus sighed. "The boy's got the miner's head. That's why we brought him along." He was visibly disappointed. "So, Arliss, you say we've been making good time in the wrong direction?"

"Yes sir," answered Arliss. "If this path doesn't turn south and west soon, we're not going to make it in time."

The miners looked at one another in gloomy silence. Their good cheer was extinguished. "Cheer up, boys," said Gustus, as jauntily as he could. "We got plenty of fire left before it's time to turn around. Meantime, there's only one way to go. So let's go." He forged ahead, in the opposite direction of where they knew their destination to be. The miner-scouts followed, but their tension grew with every step.

The miners had just lit a new pair of torches—their fourth—when they faced their first real navigational choice. A tunnel coming in from the left joined the corridor they had been following. Gustus stood in the intersection of the two passages. "Which way, Arliss?" he asked.

Arliss stood beside his foreman. "The big passage is pointing northwest. This new one points southwest."

A cheer erupted and echoed around the limestone walls. They all knew they needed to turn southwest eventually. "Hurrah!" shouted Clayton, patting Arliss on the back as he squeezed past him to lead the way down the new passage. Falling in behind him, the rest of the party broke into happy song:

Fol de rol de rol de fol de rol de rol
De fol de rol de fiddely fol de rol.

"Stop!" The miners' singing was interrupted by a shout from Arliss, who still stood in the intersection of the two passageways.

The surprised miners looked quizzically at their young comrade. He stood with his shoulders slumped and his eyes averted, the posture of a person with sad news to tell. "That's not the way."

Gustus looked at him, confused. "Pardon?"

"That's not the way, sir."

"But you said this way goes southwest," spluttered Clayton. "The Pyrthen camp lies southwest of here. That's one of the few things we know for sure."

"It's a dead end," said Arliss. "I can feel it."

"Oh no," groaned Ernest. "It's the miner's head again."

Clayton moved toward Arliss. His thick hand was clinched into a fist. "I think it's time I knocked some sense into that miner's head."

Gustus quickly stepped between them. "Tamp it down, Clayton. Everybody's feeling a little sharpish. Let's hear what the boy has to say." He turned to Arliss. "What do you mean you 'feel' a dead end?"

"You remember the long shaft at the Greasy Cave mines?"

"Since long before you was born," answered Clayton.

"It's got two entrances—north and south—and the main tunnel runs between them."

"Right," answered Gustus.

"Then there's spur shafts running off to the left and right."

"Right."

"Get to the point, boy." Clayton was losing patience.

"The point is," continued Arliss, "the air feels different in the main tunnel than it does in the spurs. The air in the spur shafts is a little staler. In the main tunnel, there's the slightest movement of air."

He took a few steps down the southward tunnel. "Here the air is dead, like a spur shaft." He stepped back into the main corridor. "Here I can feel just a tiny bit of air current."

The rest of the miner-scouts stepped back into the main corridor.

"I don't feel any difference," Clayton grumbled.

"I don't know," offered Cedric. "It might be a little fresher out here. But I wouldn't bet on it either way."

Aidan, for his part, couldn't tell any difference. It all felt dank and musty to him.

"Gustus, what do you think?" asked Ernest. "You're the foreman of this outfit."

"Don't much matter what I think about air currents and stale air," answered Gustus. "Don't imagine I could tell the difference. But I do know we brought Arliss because he's got the miner's head." Clayton groaned at this. Gustus flashed a sharp look in his direction, then continued. "More than once, his daddy's instincts got me out of scrapes down in the mines. Some folks is just born to be underground. Arliss and his family is about half-mole. So if Arliss don't feel good about that passage, I don't feel good about it. We'll carry on the way we've been going."

"You can't mean it!" shouted Clayton, his voice echoing around the cavern. "That tunnel points in the direction where we know the Pyrthen camp to be. And you're going to send us in the opposite direction because of this boy's hocus-pocus?"

Gustus answered Clayton's outburst with a quiet question. "What makes you think that tunnel leads southwest?"

Clayton saw he was trapped. Gustus pressed the point. "I want you to tell me how you know that passage leads southwest and this one leads northwest."

Clayton answered without looking at anyone. "Because Arliss said so."

"Because Arliss said so," repeated Gustus. "Without Arliss here, we wouldn't even have sense enough to know if this was north, south, east, or west. So if you've still got a hankering to explore that tunnel, go ahead. We'll pick you up on our way back. But the rest of us are going this way."

Gustus shouldered his pack and led the way northward again. And Clayton, who fell into step with the rest of the group, wasn't the only miner-scout who looked back wistfully at the southward passage as it melted into blackness.

Chapter Twenty-Five

A Very Dark Swim

It wasn't long before even Arliss had reason to doubt the wisdom of their chosen path. As they made their way along the edge of the underground lake, the shore disappeared. Sheer cliffs dropped directly into the water on either side. Gustus stood at the very last bit of shoreline and scratched his head underneath his miner's helmet. "All right, boys, we're going to have to swim for it." He had, at least, had the foresight to select for the mission only men who could swim, not a common skill among miners. "Everybody pull out your hardtack and eat what you can. I don't know how far we'll have to swim—I can't see around this bend. You're going to need your energy. Besides," he continued, "you won't be able to keep it dry, so you might as well eat it now rather than see it ruined."

The men pulled the hard biscuits out of their packs and ate hungrily. "Cedric, Ernest," Gustus continued, "can you swim with one hand and hold a torch with the other?" Both men said that they could.

"It won't ruin the extra torches if they get wet," observed Gustus. "We can shake most of the water out, and the pitch will burn in any case. But we can't let the tinder get wet. Arliss, is that tinderbox still in your pack?"

"Yes sir," the young miner answered.

"Take off your helmet, put the tinderbox on top of your head, and strap your helmet down tight over it, like this." Gustus demonstrated with his own helmet and tinderbox.

"Aidan, you a strong swimmer?" asked the old miner.

"Yes sir, pretty strong."

Gustus pulled a third tinderbox out of his pack and tossed it to Aidan. "Then you keep this one under your helmet. We've got to keep these tinderboxes dry. Do not, do *not*, *do not* let your heads go under."

Aidan strapped the tinderbox under his helmet. He found it none too comfortable. By this time, Gustus had slid into the lake and was holding Cedric's torch while Cedric got in. Aidan followed, then Arliss and the other two miners. The water was the exact same temperature as the air, but it felt a lot colder—miserably cold at first. Nevertheless, it was a relief to their sore feet to be relieved of the strain of walking on the stone and mud.

There was no telling how deep the water was, and Aidan tried not to imagine what sort of eyeless monsters might be lurking in its depths. He tried not to think about how such a creature might arise from a long sleep, awakened by the unfamiliar sound of six tasty Corenwalders thrashing around in his lake. And he refused to speculate as to how many miner-scouts such a creature could swallow in a single bite—or how many it would take to satisfy its long-dormant appetite.

He just swam, staying as close to his comrades as possible. The company had hoped that the sheer rock on either side of the lake would soon yield again to sloping banks, but the men were disappointed. The little halo of the dim torches revealed nothing but looming cliffs on either side.

They swam on in silence, clustered around the torches held aloft by Cedric and Ernest. They settled into a steady rhythm and seemed to be making decent time. But though nobody said anything, they all wondered how much farther they would have to swim—and how long they could go before reaching the point of exhaustion.

The silence was suddenly broken by a terrified yelp, which was immediately drowned out by the sound of violent splashing. Just as suddenly, it grew darker. Turning toward the sound, Aidan saw a flailing hand break the water's surface, still clutching a doused torch. Then, in the gloomy light of the one remaining torch, Ernest's face appeared, eyes bulging in panic, mouth wide in a desperate gasp, then disappeared again beneath the frothing water.

Clayton and Cedric swam to their old friend's side, and the next time he came up for air, they each grabbed an arm. In the ensuing flurry, Cedric's torch went under, too, and the party found itself in total blackness. Above the thrashing and splashing came the clear voice of Gustus: "Clayton! Cedric!"

"Sir!"

"Sir!"

"Do you have hold of Ernest?"

"We've got him," Clayton's voice came spluttering back, "but I don't know how much longer."

"Ernest?" called Gustus, struggling to stay calm.

He was answered by a spew of water, then the high, pained voice of Ernest: "It's a cramp! Can't swim!"

By this time, Aidan had swum to the near wall and found a narrow handhold. "I'm on the wall," he called into the darkness. "Gustus, Arliss, let's make a chain out to them."

Zeroing in on Aidan's voice, Gustus and Arliss found him and joined hands, Aidan anchored to the rock, Arliss in the middle, Gustus sweeping his free hand out into the darkness toward the sound of splashing. He grabbed an arm as it flailed by and tugged the whole mass of struggling, thrashing miners to safety.

Soon all six members of the party were clinging to the rock face. Out of immediate danger, Ernest was able to relax enough so that the cramp released its wrenching grip on his leg.

"Well, boys, what now?" It was Cedric's voice.

The silence and the blackness pressed down like a weight as each member of the party waited for somebody else to answer.

Gustus finally spoke. "Ernest, how you doing?"

Ernest's answer was indignant. "We ain't turning back on my account, if that's what you're thinking!"

Another long pause bore down on them as Gustus thought things over. "No fire," he said, half to himself, "and we're not sure we're going to be able to get any."

"But that's not much of a reason to turn back now," offered Clayton. "If we got no fire, we don't have much hope of making it back anyway."

Cedric spoke up: "I say we just follow this wall until we find a getting-out place, or until we just can't follow it no farther."

They all agreed to Cedric's plan. If they found a way

out of the lake and they could light their torches, the mission would go on. Otherwise, they would try to make their way back to the Corenwalder camp, one way or another.

So they continued their unlikely journey, half-swimming, feeling their way along a limestone wall in perfect darkness, calling to one another at frequent intervals to ensure that no one got separated from the party.

‡ ‡ ‡

It was difficult to gauge time in the cave, where time was not measured by the movement of sun or stars, but by the nearly constant *drip . . . drip . . . drip* that gave shape to everything in the world beneath the world. The burning of torches had given the miner-scouts a rough idea of the time they had spent in the cave, but they had no idea how long they had been creeping along the rock wall in the darkness. It might have been a couple of hours. It might have been shorter or, for that matter, much longer.

Aidan was famished, growing weaker by the minute. It wasn't only hunger and fatigue that drained him but the darkness itself, which seemed determined to swallow every spark of hope he could generate. His hands had grown soft from soaking in the water; the abrasive stone was painful to his fingertips. His helmet—or, more particularly, the tinderbox underneath his helmet—had grown especially irksome. He had even managed to swim blisters on his feet, the result of swimming in boots.

The whole group had grown sullen. The darkness had obviously done its work on the miner-scouts too. It seemed an hour since anyone had spoken a word. Then, up at the front of the line, Gustus bellowed in pain, "Aaaargh! My knee!" In the darkness, the travelers all piled into one another, unaware that their leader had stopped, lodged against an outcropping of stone just below the water's surface.

The old miner was more surprised than hurt by the collision, and he forgot all about the pain in his knee when he realized that the ledge became a gently sloping shelf rising out of the water and offering a dry surface to stand on. The whole party scrambled out of the water, rejoicing to be on dry land.

"Tinderboxes!" whooped Gustus. And before Aidan could even get his helmet off, he heard the *tchk . . . tchk . . . tchk* of flint on steel.

"Shake a torch dry!" ordered Gustus, as he continued clicking away with the flint. The flying sparks were a welcome sight to eyes accustomed to total darkness. The tinder caught, then the fat lighter, and as Gustus scooped the burning splinter into Cedric's torch, the miners dared to hope that their mission might be completed after all. Nestled in the still-damp fibers of the cane torch, the flame guttered and smoked, and Aidan felt his heart in his throat. But the pine pitch embedded in the stringy cane innards popped to light, and a little halo of light revealed that the stone they stood on was more than only a little shelf but a broad passageway where all six could walk abreast if they chose.

As Gustus was lighting a second torch, Arliss gave them the best news they had heard in many hours: The passage led south, back toward the Pyrthen camp.

Clayton clasped Arliss in a bear hug that lifted him off the ground: "Hurrah for the miner's head!" he whooped.

Energized by their improved prospects, and also worried that their torches wouldn't last, they made their way down the passage at a brisk pace, almost at a trot.

"How much fire we got left?" asked Ernest, who had long since recovered from his cramp.

"Let's see . . ." said Gustus, stroking his beard. "We started with twenty pair. That was the seventh pair that you and Clayton lost in the water. These are the eighth pair. Two more pair after these, and we turn it around."

"Step it up, boys," called Arliss. "No time to waste!"

They were almost running now down the broad corridor, and they sang their high-spirited caving song:

Oh, the miners brave of Greasy Cave,
Came out the other side.
They braved the gloom, they challenged doom,
They made an end to Pyrthen pride.
Fol de rol de rol de fol de rol de rol
De fol de rol de fiddely fol de rol.

The ninth pair of torches was burning when Arliss noticed something odd on the ceiling above them. It looked like a twisted mass of gigantic snakes spiraling out thirty feet or more, branching and intertwining. Arliss nudged Aidan and pointed upward. "Tree roots," he observed. "We must be getting near the surface."

Cedric looked up too. "That's not a little tree either," he observed. "Look at the size of those roots."

Aidan stopped short. "We're in the middle of a plain. There aren't many trees."

"Not that size anyway," offered Arliss.

"There are a few big pine trees and a few big cedars."

Gustus craned his neck to study the root system. "I've tunneled under many a pine tree. Those aren't pine roots. Not cedar either. That's a hardwood."

"A hardwood!" shouted Arliss excitedly. "There ain't but one big hardwood within eyeshot of camp. That's the live oak the giant used to stand by every afternoon."

"So we're . . ." Aidan began.

"We're standing underneath the Pyrthen camp!" shouted Gustus. "We're almost there!"

"And not a minute too soon," observed Clayton as the torch in his hand guttered out. They lit a tenth pair of torches—their last before they would have to turn back—and pressed on.

Five minutes later, the passageway narrowed to a tight crevice. Gustus held his torch to the crevice and tried to peer through. He looked down at his broad chest and shook his head. He turned sideways and leaned into the crack. He groaned and pushed with his legs, but it was clear to everyone that there was no use.

"You'd have to be an eel to get through that hole," he sighed dejectedly. "We've come so far." His voice cracked with emotion. He buried his head in his hands. "So far . . ."

Aidan stepped up to the crevice. "Sir?" he asked. "Gustus? Mind if I give it a try?"

Gustus looked up. His wet eyes glistened in the torch-light. "Sure, son," he answered, trying to smile. "That's why we brought you, isn't it? To squeeze into spots where old fat miners can't go."

Aidan sidled into the crack, a torch in his lead hand, his pack swung around to his trailing shoulder. It was a tight fit. It grew tighter as he progressed through the crevice. As the walls closed in, he could feel panic rising in his gorge. He heard Arliss's voice behind him: "If you're stuck, breathe out. Don't hold your breath."

It went against his instincts, but Aidan did as Arliss said; Arliss did, after all, have the miner's head. He blew out steadily and felt his chest contract just enough to dislodge him. Then, before he realized what had happened, he popped through to the other side. To his surprise, Arliss was right behind him.

"Thought I'd have a look too," Arliss explained.

"How in the world did you get through?" asked Aidan, for though Arliss was the skinniest of the miners, he was still bigger than Aidan.

"One more bite of hardtack, and I couldn't have made it," grinned Arliss.

Where they stood, the cave broadened again. They were facing due west.

"Do you smell that?" asked Arliss. Since they had gone underground, they had smelled nothing but that damp, earthy smell. Now, for the first time, they smelled something else, and this aroma was unmistakable. It was the sharp, sweet, smoky smell that drifted over when the Pyrthens fired their thunder-tubes.

From the other side of the crevice came the voice of Gustus. "Arliss? Aidan? What do you see?"

Arliss called back through the crack, "I think we've made it! We can smell the smoke of the Pyrthen thunder-tubes, and we have a broad tunnel leading west." Aidan and Arliss heard the sounds of celebration on the other side of the crevice. But the celebration quickly subsided, and the miner-scouts were talking business again.

"Fresh torch!" called Cedric, and Aidan noticed that his own torch was getting close to the end too. That would be the eleventh pair—the end of the road.

Gustus's voice came calling through the crevice. "Come on back, boys!"

Arliss looked at Aidan in horror. To have come so close just to turn around!

They heard Gustus speaking to his comrades. He had shaken off the gloom he felt when he had gotten stuck at the mouth of the crevice. "Limestone's soft. And it breaks off in pretty big chunks. We should be able to cut a path big enough for a troop of lightly armed soldiers in a matter of hours.

"But not now," he continued. "Fire's half gone. We got to get back. Boys!" he shouted. "You coming or not?"

Aidan and Arliss didn't answer. They heard the voice of Clayton. "Seems a shame not to let them look around a few minutes. They're that close."

Gustus was firm. "No. From the start I said we'd turn around when we lit the eleventh pair of torches, even if we could smell the Pyrthens. This part of the mission is over. We found the passage. But what good does that do if we don't get back to camp with the news?"

Aidan and Arliss pressed their ears to the crack, straining to hear every word. "Tomorrow," continued Gustus, "we come back with a whole troop of soldiers and as many torches as they can carry. Aidan! Arliss!" he bellowed, "you're about to get left!"

"I'm not going back," whispered Aidan. Arliss stared at him. "I'm going to see the Pyrthen end of this cave with my own eyes. Are you with me?"

Arliss was obviously torn. He wanted to continue the mission as badly as Aidan did. But he had never disobeyed Gustus. "He's my foreman. And he's the best foreman that ever wore a miner's helmet."

"You're not a miner anymore, Arliss. You're a scout. If they're going to the camp and coming back here, they don't need our help. They know the way now."

"But I didn't bring torches or tinder," whispered Arliss, but he was only making excuses now.

"I've got two torches and a tinderbox. That leaves the rest of the company with two tinderboxes and more than enough torches."

"Arliss!" came Gustus's voice, angry now.

"Here's the thing," whispered Aidan, "they can't get back here with a troop of soldiers until sometime tomorrow, maybe even the next day. If the Pyrthens fire up those thunder-tubes again, there may not be a tomorrow for the Corenwalder army. In the meantime, there's a tiny little chance that we can do some good on this end."

"Arliss! Aidan!" Gustus was furious now.

"I'm sorry, sir," called Arliss into the crack. "We aren't coming back."

"I ain't asking, Arliss! I'm giving you an order!"

But Aidan and Arliss had already started making their way down the passage toward the Pyrthen camp.

Chapter Twenty-Six

Powder and Dust

As Aidan and Arliss moved westward along the edge of another underground pool, the smell of the thunder-tubes grew stronger. They hadn't gone far when Aidan saw up ahead a patch of gray, hovering high in the middle distance. Arliss saw it, too, and as they moved closer, they glimpsed a twinkle of light and realized they were seeing a sliver of the night sky.

"We've made it through," Arliss gasped. "We've made it through!"

"Shhhh!" hissed Aidan. He was as eager as Arliss, but that glimpse of sky reminded him that they were very close to the world where Pyrthens stalked, and he had no desire to attract their attention.

They crept closer to the entrance, through a narrow neck that opened into a small chamber. The floor of the chamber sloped up to a jagged hole, about six feet across, that opened up to the starlit heavens.

Aidan and Arliss stood gazing at the sky. It had only been a few hours since they had last seen it, but in that short span there had been many moments when they had doubted they would ever see the sky again.

"What next?" whispered Aidan.

Arliss was a few feet away, just out of the torchlight,

looking at something that Aidan couldn't make out in the darkness.

"Pssst!" whispered Arliss. "Bring the torch."

When Aidan got closer with the torch, he saw what Arliss was looking at: dozens of barrels stacked against the cave wall.

"So the Pyrthens are using the cave as a storeroom," whispered Aidan. "Just like Harlan's family did. Good place for it, I guess. Nice and cool. What are these, ale barrels?"

"That's not ale we're smelling," Arliss remarked. He pointed at the ground near one of the barrels, where a little black spot stood in stark contrast to the white clay. "What you suppose that is?"

Aidan swung the torch in the direction of the spot where Arliss pointed. As he did, a bit of torch pitch popped and sent a shower of orange sparks in all directions.

Ka-poppp!

The little black spot on the ground exploded in a blaze of white light that blinded Aidan and Arliss and threw up a plume of white smoke that enveloped them in the sweet, acrid smell they knew from the Pyrthen thunder-tubes. Aidan's ears rang. He could see nothing but bright spots of color swirling in front of him.

When the thud of heavy boots echoed in the cave entrance, Aidan barely had the presence of mind to react. He snatched off his helmet and put it over the torch to kill the flame. Then he grabbed Arliss, who hadn't moved since the fire flash, and pulled him behind a barrel.

A Pyrthen soldier, fully uniformed and armed, burst through the cave entrance bearing a flaming torch. "Who's there?" he growled, scanning the chamber. But his eyes weren't adjusted to the profound darkness, and he didn't see the two Corenwalders who peered at him from behind the barrel.

The torchbearer was followed almost immediately by a second soldier, who pulled off his own helmet and killed the torch flame, just as Aidan had his own.

"Hey," began the first soldier, "what's the big . . ."

"Idiot!" snapped the second soldier, cutting him short. "You know not to come in here with a flame!"

"But I heard a pop, and I smelled smoke, and I . . ."

"If you touch off that flame powder, we'll hear a pop like the world has never heard before!" He pointed at the barrels stacked along the wall. "That's enough flame powder for enough cannon shots to conquer this pitiful little country ten times over. One little spark is enough to set the whole thing off."

"I just thought . . ." began the first soldier. He was shaking now, terrified at the thought of what his carelessness might have led to.

"We've been guarding this cave entrance all night," said the second soldier. "There's nobody in here." He pointed out the cave entrance. "Look, it's getting light out. Our watch is over. It'll be less than an hour before the cannon fire begins again. Let's try to get some rest."

The Pyrthens heaved themselves out of the cave, leaving Aidan and Arliss in the darkness. "Flame powder?" whispered Arliss. "What's flame powder?"

"It must be what makes the thunder-tubes boom," answered Aidan. He looked in awe at the stacked barrels. "And that's tons of it."

Arliss thought back to the little explosion that had so

stunned them minutes before. "How much flame powder made that flash a minute ago?"

"It would fit into the palm of your hand," said Aidan.

"Then that's enough flame powder to . . ." Arliss shivered to think about what that much powder could do.

Aidan finished his sentence: "Enough to put an end to Corenwald." The boys sat glumly in the dim light that made its way in from the brightening sky outside.

A strange light was visible in Aidan's eyes, even in the dimness of the cave. He reached into his pack and pulled out the tinderbox. "It's also enough to put an end to an invading army!" Before Arliss knew what was happening, he heard the *tchk . . . tchk . . . tchk . . . tchk . . . tchk . . .* of Aidan madly striking flint on steel. Sparks were flying at the dry tinder.

"Hold on there, big boy!" whispered Arliss as he snatched up the tinder. "Let's think on this a minute. I ain't opposed to blowing up the Pyrthens, but if we can do it without blowing up our own selves, I'd rather do it that way."

"What do you suggest then?" asked Aidan, his eyes still flashing.

"You're a farm boy, right?" asked Arliss.

"Yes," answered Aidan, "what about it?"

"You ever do a straight burn?"

"Sure. Every winter."

"I saw a farmer near Greasy Cave do it once. He made a narrow little line of fire go straight from one end of the field to the other. I never knew how he did it."

"It's not hard," said Aidan. "You just pour a line of turpentine where you want fire to go, put a flame to it, and there it goes."

217

"I was just wondering, could we do a straight burn that runs from back there somewhere"—Arliss pointed in the direction they had come from—"maybe that little pool—to these barrels? We could pour a line of flame powder instead of turpentine, put fire to it at the far end, and be a long way off when the barrels boom."

Aidan grinned and pounded Arliss on the back. "Arliss, you're a genius."

Arliss tapped his helmet.

"I know," said Aidan. "It's the miner's head."

"Our best bet is to get into that pool if we can," remarked Arliss. "I don't know what kind of fire we're about to let loose, but I doubt even flame powder can burn water."

"Good plan," agreed Aidan. "The Pyrthen guards said they'd start firing in an hour. We better move fast."

Enough daylight found its way in for the boys to work. The seal was broken on one of the barrels, and they managed to tip it over. The powder fuse would lead there. Using their helmets for scoops, they poured a thick rope of powder along the cave floor as far as the squeeze that served as the cavern's back door.

The task got much harder once they were into the next chamber, for the sunlight didn't reach there. They couldn't safely light their torch, so they felt their way in the dark.

They were only a few steps beyond the squeeze when they heard a faint *boom* from outside, followed by another and another. "The thunder-tubes!" said Aidan in a hoarse whisper. "They're firing again." He thought of the terror of his countrymen, the helplessness they felt against such weapons.

"If they're firing those thunder-tubes," observed Arliss, "it won't be long before somebody comes down here for more powder. We're out of time, Aidan. We've got to touch this thing off."

"You're right," answered Aidan. "But let's be smart about it. How much powder is left in your helmet?"

"Two or three heavy handfuls, I'd say."

"Mine's almost half full. We've got to empty these helmets. But we can't just dump them out. It has to be a nice, even line like we've been making."

Boom! Boom! Boom!

"Aidan!" shouted Arliss. "We've got to light this thing! We got no more time!"

Boom! Boom!

"All right," agreed Aidan. He put the tinderbox and a wood splinter in Arliss's hands. "You step off ten or twelve strides and light this splinter. Hand me your helmet. I'll finish the powder line while you're making fire."

Boom! Boom! Boom!

Aidan bent to his work, trying to ignore the booming of the thunder-tubes. This was a crucial part of the task. At the other end, the powder line was thick and ropelike; big fire was good as the fuse approached the powder barrels. But at this end, they needed a controlled fire; they wanted to blow up the barrels without blowing themselves up. In near-total darkness, with the booming of thunder-tubes overhead and the threat of Pyrthens uncovering their plot any second, it was hard for Aidan to create the narrow, even powder line he needed.

Boom! Boom! Boom!

Tchk ... tchk ... tchk.

Arliss was striking away with the flint.

Tchk ... tchk ... tchk.

Aidan could feel the nervous sweat dripping down the slope of his nose. He had emptied Arliss's helmet, but there was still a couple of handfuls of powder left in his own.

Boom! Boom! Boom!

Tchk ... tchk ... tchk.

Then, from the entry chamber, he heard the shuffle of boots and a murmur of voices.

"Hurry!" he whispered at Arliss.

Tchk ... tchk ... tchk ... tchk ... tchk.

The tinder wouldn't catch.

From the next chamber came a Pyrthen voice. "Oy! Freymerge! What's this?"

"What's what?" asked another Pyrthen.

"This line of flame powder!" Aidan could hear the soldiers' footsteps coming toward them as they followed the powder line.

Boom! Boom! Boom!

Tchk ... tchk ... tchk.

Aidan trailed out the last of the powder from his helmet. "Arliss," he whispered, "forget the tinder. Bring the flint."

Arliss squatted beside him, flint in hand. It suddenly grew completely dark in the chamber; the few rays of light coming in through the rock squeeze were blocked by the form of a soldier trying to squeeze through.

"Fly, Pyrthen!" called Aidan. "Fly! We're lighting the

flame powder. Get out!" The soldier stopped, but he didn't run away.

Boom! Boom! Boom!

"Get him!" came the panicked voice of the other Pyrthen. "Stop him!" Aidan and Arliss could hear the soldier grunting as he tried to push through the narrow space.

"He had his chance," Aidan whispered to Arliss.

Tchk . . . tchk . . . tchk . . . tchk.

The intermittent flash of flint sparks gave Arliss enough light to find the end of the powder trail.

Tchk.

The powder caught and hissed to life. By the white flash they saw the terror-stricken face of the Pyrthen soldier, who turned and fled from the sparkling fire that came racing toward him.

Aidan scooped up the two helmets and stuck one on his own head, the other on Arliss's. Still seeing spots, the boys stumbled toward the safety of the pool.

They were no sooner in the water than the cave shook with the force of an earthquake. The cavern grew bright, lit by a fire that shot through the squeeze. The boys pressed themselves against the pool's rock wall, terrified by what they had unleashed. A hail of rocks, some quite large, rocketed over their heads, propelled by an explosion that rumbled on for half a minute as one barrel of powder touched off the barrels next to it in a chain of explosions that grew stronger and stronger before finally settling down.

Even after the explosion stopped, huge chunks of stone continued to fall, thudding to the cave floor and rocking the pool into high waves that tossed Aidan and Arliss around like chips of driftwood in a stormy sea and finally threw them out of the water and onto the pool's rocky bank.

Bruised and terribly sore, Aidan lay on the jagged stone, spluttering and coughing in the darkness. The air was so thick with dust that it was hardly more breathable than the water he had just escaped. A few feet away, Arliss was hacking and spitting. In a brief pause between coughing fits, Aidan heard Arliss's voice, muffled but urgent: "Breathe through your tunic!"

"Pardon?" Aidan's mouth and throat were so gummy with inhaled cave dust that he could hardly speak the word.

"Pull your tunic over your mouth and nose and breathe through it"—Arliss was interrupted by another violent coughing fit—"or this dust will choke you."

Aidan did as Arliss instructed. The tunic mask filtered out just enough dust for Aidan to get his breath. But both boys continued hacking and coughing so hard that they could hardly carry on a conversation.

"Can you walk?" called Aidan into the darkness.

"I think so," answered Arliss, grunting a little as he picked himself up. "Can you?"

Aidan struggled to his feet. Everything hurt, but nothing seemed to be broken. "I think so."

Their one exit was blocked. A single spot of light illuminated the suspended cave dust where the rock squeeze used to lead to the entry chamber. "We're buried," observed Arliss. "If we can't dig our way out, we aren't getting out."

On hands and knees, Aidan and Arliss crawled

painfully over loose, jagged rock toward the little slit of light, their only hope of ever seeing the sky again. Arliss pulled a chunk of limestone out of the rubble pile that blocked the cave neck, and the tiny ray became a small shaft of light, no thicker than a finger. Aidan's eyes filled with tears of gratitude as he looked along the ray that shot past him into the cave's deeper darkness. He caught the streaming light in his hand as if it were a stream of water. Never had he been so happy to see a shaft of light and floating dust.

Forgetting about the pains in his arms, his legs, his back, his side, his neck, and his head, Aidan attacked the rubble pile. He wanted more light. He had to see more light!

"Whoa!" shouted Arliss. "Careful now!"

But is was too late. The first rock Aidan pulled out caused a collapse and a little landslide that blocked out what little light they had. They found themselves in darkness again.

"Why don't you let me do this?" suggested Arliss. Aidan watched intently for another sliver of light as Arliss worked methodically at the rubble pile. Soon a new ray of light appeared, then another, then another as Arliss cleared stone and pebbles away.

Before long, Arliss had opened a tiny passage through the rubble, and on their bellies the boys squeezed through to the entry chamber—or what used to be the entry chamber. It was now an enormous crater. Its roof had been blown off by the exploding fire powder and was open to the morning sky.

Chapter Twenty-Seven

A Battle, A Rout

idan and Arliss stood on the crater floor, blinking against the intensity of the morning sun. Above them, a huge column of smoke hung in the sky. The smell of fire and destruction was heavy in the air. In the distance they could hear the thundering of horses' hooves, the clash of steel on steel, the shouts and groans of men doing battle.

The boys picked their way to the crater's edge and peered out, taking care to avoid notice. But there was little need of that. The camp was deserted. The crater was the center of a circle of utter destruction. The Pyrthens' supply depot had been in this vicinity—all their food, the fodder for their horses and mules, their arms and armor. Overturned wagons, many of them still burning, lay scattered about. The ground was littered with smoking bits of twisted plate armor and shattered spears and battle-axes.

"Where is everybody?" whispered Arliss. Aidan pointed toward the west. The Pyrthens were fleeing westward across the plain, toward Middenmarsh and their transport ships. The Corenwalder army was in hot pursuit.

Taking advantage of the chaos that followed the explosion in the Pyrthen camp, King Darrow had led a charge across the valley and put the invaders to flight. Now, astride his foaming warhorse, he thundered across the plain at the head of his army. This was the picture of King Darrow that Aidan carried in his heart. This was the Darrow whom Aidan had been taught to love and revere. The Corenwalders who followed him into battle remembered for the first time in a long time why this Darrow had been chosen to be their king, and they were ennobled by the very sight of him.

Both boys wanted badly to catch up to their army, but neither was in any shape to run across the plain. Across the way Aidan spotted a pack mule still tethered to a hitching post. "Come on," he shouted to Arliss. The two boys clambered out of the crater and ran toward the skittish animal. They untied the lead rope and both climbed onto the mule's bare back.

In the far distance, the leading edge of the Pyrthen army was melting into the forest of the Eechihoolee River bottom, which formed the western boundary of the Bonifay Plain. Aidan and Arliss urged their mount onward, but the poor mule was a beast of burden not a warhorse, and they never managed to go any faster than a trot. They were still a quarter-league away when the last of the Pyrthen soldiers disappeared into the tangled forest.

The Corenwalders didn't follow the invaders into the woods. King Darrow halted his fighting men on the verge of the forest. When Aidan and Arliss caught up, the king was arranging the soldiers into a long line. His answer to the Pyrthens' terrified, disorganized flight would be a disciplined, methodical sweep through the forest.

But the army's reformation was interrupted by a distant eruption of wild animal calls from the depths of the forest:

Ha-ha-ha-hrawffff-wooooooooo . . . Ha-ha-ha-hrawffff-wooooooooo.

Ha-ha-ha-hrawffff-wooooooooo . . . Ha-ha-ha-hrawffff-wooooooooo.

Haaaaaaawwwwwweeeeeeee!

Ha-ha-ha-hrawffff-wooooooooo . . . Ha-ha-ha-hrawffff-wooooooooo.

Haaaaaaawwwwwweeeeeeee!

Haaaaaaawwwwwweeeeeeee!

These peculiar sounds were immediately followed by thousands of panicked screams. And then, to the Corenwalders' amazement, they were overrun by Pyrthens coming back out of the woods. The same soldiers who had run into the forest to escape the Corenwalders were now running headlong toward them. But this was a surrender not a counterattack.

Whatever was happening in the Eechihoolee Forest, the Pyrthens found it more terrifying than the battle on the plain. Their eyes were wild with panic, their faces ghostly white. They came out of the forest with their hands raised, to show that they had thrown down their weapons.

The Corenwalders could make little sense of the Pyrthens' garbled accounts of what happened in the forest. Some sort of mass hysteria had obviously befallen them, probably brought on by the shock of the flame powder explosion and the added stress of their flight across the plain. They babbled about "lizard men" and "gray people" and "tree alligators" that had attacked them from the treetops and from underwater when they reached the river in the middle of the forest. It was as if, in their hour of panic, their minds reverted to the fairy tales and scary stories that old people and nursemaids tell about the feechiefolk.

Aidan chuckled and spoke to himself: "Our fights is their fights, and their fights is our'n."

"What's that?" asked Arliss, who still sat behind him on the mule.

"Oh, nothing," answered Aidan. "I was just remembering something a friend told me."

Epilogue

Back at Longleaf

Summer was drawing to a close. In the orchard, the apples and pears were beginning to take shape. The sheep's wool was just beginning to thicken. The meadow grass was turning yellow, exhausted from months of summer sun.

And Aidan Errolson, Corenwald's deliverer, was back in the bottom pasture, tending his sheep. "What's a fellow got to do to get respect around here?" he grumbled as he untangled a lamb from a blackberry bush. He deepened his voice in imitation of Bayard the Truthspeaker. "'Live the life that unfolds before you.' That's easy for him to say. He and his goats go where they please. The only thing unfolding before me is more work."

"Baaahhhh," said the lamb.

"Oh, so you're on their side, are you? Maybe you'd like to have a nice Pyrthen shepherd watching you. And a nice Pyrthen family in the manor house. And a nice Pyrthen tyrant living in Tambluff Castle."

"Baaaahhhh!" said the lamb a little louder, for the blackberry thorns were pricking her.

"Well, next time there's a giant threatening to enslave the whole country, maybe you'd like to go slay him. Because I'm through with it. I'm telling you, I'm—"

Aidan stopped himself. "Oh, good grief. I'm as bad as Bayard, talking to livestock."

He went back to his work. When the lamb was free, Aidan heard the slow creak of wagon wheels coming from the next pasture. Watching the cart path, he saw two golden plumes come bobbing over the rise, attached to the gleaming bridles of two magnificent draft horses. They pulled a long, low wagon draped with blue silk embroidered with the golden boar.

Running toward the wagon, Aidan saw that the driver was Wendell, the royal gamekeeper. He also recognized the riders who came over the rise behind the wagon: his father Errol and King Darrow.

"Aidan, we've brought an old friend of yours," said King Darrow. "We thought it was time he came home."

"Climb on the driver's bench with Wendell," Errol directed his son, "and show him how to get to the river beside the indigo field."

With Aidan's help, Wendell maneuvered the big wagon to the riverbank. Errol and Darrow followed close behind. When everyone had dismounted, Wendell pulled the drape from the wagon. There, inside his heavy iron cage, was Samson the alligator. He had been snoozing under the drape, and he was furious at Wendell for disturbing him. He opened his terrible jaws and hissed menacingly. He thrashed his tail a couple of times and lunged at Aidan with a bellow that echoed over the river.

"Hey, that's my boy!" cheered Aidan. "That's my boy!" He clapped for Samson's impressive demonstration. Here was Corenwald in all its primeval energy—the Corenwald of old, the Corenwald yet to be.

Samson almost looked his old self again. A few streaks of gold paint lingered in the crevices between his scales, but for the most part he looked just the way he did when Aidan first saw him.

"After the treaty feast," said King Darrow, "the Pyrthens left in such a hurry that they didn't bother to take home their . . . *ahem* . . . party favor." The king looked almost sheepish as he gestured at Samson.

"But how did you get the paint off him?" Aidan asked.

Wendell laughed. "He did that by himself. I just turned him loose in the Tambluff moat, and he wallowed it off."

Wendell opened the cage door and prodded the alligator's tail with a pole. Samson slid out of the cage and into the water. For a few seconds he floated like a bumpy log, eyeing his captors. Then he disappeared under the water.

"He seems glad to be home," remarked King Darrow, watching the alligator's tail ripples dissipate across the water's surface. Then he turned to Aidan. "And what about you, Aidan? Are you glad to be home?"

Aidan paused for a second or two before answering. "Yes, Your Majesty . . . I'm happy to be home. Of course I am." But Aidan's uncertain tone revealed more than his words.

"Aidan," continued the king, "you are no shepherd boy. You have been a faithful and obedient son to your father. But now you belong to Corenwald.

"You believed in Corenwald—and in Corenwald's God—when I, the king of Corenwald, didn't. I had forgotten many things, but you made me remember. I need to surround myself with men like you."

Aidan looked from King Darrow to his father and back again.

"Aidan," continued the king, "I want you to come live at Tambluff Castle. Join my son Steren in his study of the arts of government—law, diplomacy, warfare. Steren will be king someday, and he will need lieutenants and advisers." Darrow put a hand on Aidan's shoulder. "Aidan, you have the heart to serve Corenwald. Anyone who saw you on the Bonifay Plain knows that. I want to be sure you have the skills."

This was more than Aidan could comprehend at first. "Y-your Majesty, you're asking me to join your court?"

The king nodded his head. Aidan looked to his father.

"The king and I have discussed this at length," said Errol, in answer to his son's inquiring look. "I'll miss you terribly, son, but King Darrow is right. Go to Tambluff with my blessing. It's best for you. It's best for Corenwald."

Errol smiled at Aidan. "You've learned every lesson I've ever tried to teach you. But you have many more things to learn—things you can learn only at the court of Darrow."

"Well, that settles it, doesn't it?" said Aidan, smiling at his father and his king. "I'll pack my trunk. On to Tambluff!"